Sweet ON YOU

KC ENDERS

Print ISBN: 979-8-9911880-4-3

Sweet ON YOU

Sweet on You

She's a bubbly, sugary sweet pastry chef. Living her best
life in the Big Apple.
Luxury apartment. Successful patisserie.
Everything is great–better than great. It's absolutely
perfect.

He's grumbly and growly–and so very out of his
element–
working on a temporary assignment in NYC.
He wants to do his job and get out. Back to the clean air
in the mountains near Denver.

Throw them together.
Mix things up.
Turn up the heat and what you get is, quite simply,
alarming.

To my sweet husband. I'm so glad we're home again.

One

Raleigh

I step off the plane, and the shitstorm that will be my life for the next couple of months starts immediately. The pushing and shoving. The throngs of bodies, the elbows to the ribs, and the busted give-a-fuck. What the hell is wrong with this city?

Some dude throws his man-purse across his chest, practically hitting me upside the head in the process. *Fucking asshat.*

I mumble, "Excuse me," and get nothing but a condescending glare in return.

Side-stepping, I try to squeeze through the crush of

what looks like a bunch of lemmings blindly running for the edge of the cliff.

I hate New York City.

Take me back to Denver, to the mountains of the Pacific Northwest—anywhere but here.

I pop my earbuds in place—retreating into my own private bubble—and haul ass to baggage claim. My teeth scrape, top against the bottom ones, molars grinding to dust as I go. I have no patience for this shit, none at all. At least the music thumping through my head distracts me, keeping me sane.

To say I don't want to be here would be an understatement. Maybe the understatement of the century, but career-wise it's a solid choice.

The engineer who started the project downtown did a shit job of following protocol and it didn't take long for the whole thing to be over budget and behind schedule. Digging this project out of the shitter is a golden opportunity.

On a personal level, the break is a godsend. After the year I just closed out, I need a change of scenery, a chance to clear my head. The fact that this isn't where I want to be does not fucking matter. Not in the least.

At baggage claim, I stand back, looking over the heads of the people crowded around the belt. I murmur another useless *excuse me* when my first bag rounds the bend and then watch helplessly as it slides around another curve, disappearing back through the plastic strips. I'm used to manners, common decency—personal space.

I pride myself on using them regularly, but when I see my second bag, I push my way through to the front of the crowd and grab it off the conveyor belt. And then I stay there. I've claimed my space, and there's no way I'm letting my other bag pass me by again.

Finally—with all of my crap—I take off for the front of the terminal, trying to breathe. Not yoga breathing, or whatever the fuck, but real, actual breathing. Pulling air into my lungs and pushing it back out. The crowds and people suffocate me. The stress. I need a drink.

I check my watch and realize that—with the change in time zones—it's not too early for a beer.

I hail a cab, or I try. It takes longer than I would have thought for one to stop with the sea of dirty yellow cars stretching as far as the eye can see. When one finally pulls up in front of me, I load my bags and fold myself into the back. Anticipating a death-ride through traffic hell and into the city itself, that beer I was just considering quickly becomes a whiskey in my mind.

"Midtown. 48th and Lexington, please," I grumble.

"You here for business or pleasure?" my cab driver asks in a thick southern accent, glancing back at me in the rearview mirror.

"Business," I say, tearing my eyes from the mirror to

the bumper of the car squeezing into the lane in front of us. I swear we're going to hit it, and my eyes widen as I brace myself for impact.

Somehow my driver, Roy—according to the laminated paper bolted to the back of his seat—stops in time, just shy of hitting the car in front of us. He nods at me with a wide smile. "But you'll take in the sights, right? How can you not? The city's—"

I cut him off, hoping for a little bit of quiet after the chaos of the airport. "Doubt it. Sooner I get the job done, the sooner I get home."

Oh, how quickly I adopt that New York state of mind and the attitude that goes with it. As my shit luck would have it though, Roy is not at all fazed by my rudeness.

"You ain't gonna see a show? Tour the museums? Nothing? The Freedom Tower?"

This time, I stare straight ahead out the windshield, focusing on the sea of cars clogging every single lane into the city. I don't want to encourage him by making eye contact. "No. Work, home on a weekend every now and then. Stay on schedule and get this done."

"Not much of a city guy?" he asks, still not giving up. "Family back home in…?" The question hangs uncomfortably in the overly warm, stale air.

I blow out a breath and remind myself that this guy has been nothing but nice, and not at all what I expect from a New York City taxi driver. "Denver, and I'm really not. Mountains, hiking, wide-open spaces are my thing. I'm sure the city is great—a real treat for some—but there are too many people, you know?" I don't need to lay my entire life out for him, no matter how nice of a guy he seems to be.

Roy bobs his head. "I hear you, I hear you. Took me some adjusting—how busy it is and all—but you got to take advantage of your time here. There's nothing like it, and where you're staying, you got access to everything," he tells me, changing lanes and waving a hand to the blare of horns as he does it.

Either accepting defeat, or maybe my manners push their way back to the surface, I give in and ask, "Alabama, huh?"

"Yes, sir. Spent my whole life there working a farm, but the love of my life wanted to follow her dreams and live in the big city, so here I am, you know?" He grins wide, his head bobbing along to his words. "How'd you know it? Where I'm from and all."

"Lucky guess, I suppose," I say. "But love like that, I don't know if I believe in that anymore. I'm sure as hell not rushing into anything again. If I find someone to love, I'm taking my time with it—go about things the right way." I turn my head and scrutinize the skyline of what will be my temporary home for the next couple of months. Even the snow discarded on the side of the road looks miserable and uncomfortable.

Roy exits the massive highway and transitions seamlessly into the slow crawl across the city.

"Love absolutely is forever, and when you find it, you're a damn fool not to follow wherever it takes you." Sadness pinches at the features of his face.

I turn away again and watch as the buildings slide by. I'm pretty much done with this conversation. This is a cab ride, not a therapy session, and I sure as shit don't want to give my ex-wife any more space in my life. Our interactions will be strictly business from here on out. Or at least as much as they can be. When it comes to our son, nothing else matters. She can be as hateful as she wants, but Matty doesn't need to know the details of why his world got turned upside down. No kid needs that.

The taxi slides up to the curb outside a high-rise that matches the picture in my email. I could have expensed a hotel for the entirety of my stay, but with everything else in my life feeling so off—so temporary—I wanted something with a little more space and opted for a place to sublet.

"Here y'are," Roy drawls. "Let's get your bags out. You get yourself settled, and then you need to find you a drink—something to fortify you. Then, go out and sample the city. See what she has to offer." He pops open his door as I slide my card through the reader and pay my fare, leaving a healthy tip. He's been nothing but decent to me, and I didn't die, so there's that.

By the time my feet hit the pavement, Roy's got my bags out of the trunk and ready to go. He gives me a hearty handshake and a slap on the back. "Give her a chance to woo you. You might find a new place to call home." He has no idea just how wrong that statement is.

"Thanks for the ride." I nod, grabbing my bags off the sidewalk and maneuvering through the late afternoon commute, eager to get out of the cold because even that's different here.

And who knew that crossing nine feet of cement could be such a fucking production? I pause outside the revolving glass doors of my temporary home and mutter a curse to the engineer who designed this shit. It's excellent for pedestrian flow, and I'm sure it's aesthetically pleasing, but it's a fucking pain in the ass when you're loaded down with luggage.

"Sir?"

I glance to my right and see a gentleman holding open a glass door, his breath a visible cloud in the frigid air. "Thanks," I call to him, surprised when he takes one of the bags from my hand. "You don't have to—"

"It's no problem, sir," he answers as he pulls the door closed behind us, shutting out the damp cold. Once we're across the plush carpet and standing at a desk, he blows into his hands, rubbing them together for warmth. "Now, what can I do for you, Mr. …?"

"Jacobs. Raleigh Jacobs. I'm subletting an apartment from, uh, Kent Brown. He said to ask for Thomas," I say.

"And that would be me."

I extend my hand, and for a brief moment, Thomas stares at it as if this isn't commonplace. Or maybe he's a germaphobe—who knows? Just as I'm starting to feel like he's going to leave me hanging, he reaches out and, with a firm grip, shakes my hand.

"Let me know if there is anything I can do to help you while you're with us," he says. "Welcome home, sir."

"It's a short-term thing," I respond, huffing out a small laugh. I pocket the keys he hands me and signing the forms he placed on the counter.

"You never know," Thomas says with a smirk. "You might just fall in love with the place."

Why the hell is everyone saying that? I'm not in the market for love—not with a woman and, sure as shit, not with New York City. Matty, the mountains—I love those two things, though not equally by any account.

When I get back home, I'm getting a new dog since, in all honesty, kids and dogs are the only beings capable of unconditional love. And because Laney, my ex-wife and the Wicked Bitch of the West, kept my dog in the divorce. *My dog.* Mine.

"Sir?" Thomas's question pulls me back to the present, but obviously, I missed something.

"I'm sorry. I was…" I trail off because, really, what was I? Lost in thought? Pissed off at the world? Dreaming of seeing this city in my rearview mirror? How about all of the above?

"Not a problem. I'm sure it's been a long day of travel. I asked if you need a hand getting your things up to your apartment," Thomas kindly repeats himself.

"Thanks, but no. I've got it."

He points me toward the elevators as his desk phone rings. I wave my thanks to him and grab my bags. The silence of the elevator car is like a balm to my frayed nerves and prickly attitude, and lulls me into a false sense of security. Because as soon as the doors slide open, my teeth are back to grinding and scraping—top against bottom—reducing my molars to dust.

The smoke alarm from one of the apartments on this level is blaring its discontent.

Loudly.

Shrilly.

Any progress I made in relaxing—though the amount is negligible, I'm sure—dissipates as my shoulders tense and lift, ending up somewhere around my ears. I haul ass down the hallway, digging in the pocket of my jeans for the key I just stowed there. Unfortunately, the farther I go, the louder the brain-killing blare becomes.

I reach the door of my apartment and drop my duffle to the floor. Of course, it's the apartment right next to me. Scrambling to get the key in the lock and escape this madness, I drop the single key and watch as it disappears into the tiny gap at the end of my duffle's zipper. I'm sure I should be worried about whether the building is about to burn down with the way the alarm is screaming, but it strikes me that no one else seems to be all that bothered by it.

My search abandoned for the moment, I knock on the door of the offending apartment and wait.

And knock. And wait.

And wait.

Barely audible over the alarm, a voice calls, "I know, I know. Just use your key, Josh."

I knock again, louder this time, more insistent, and finally, the door swings open. There's no one there, just a blur of movement rushing back into the apartment and a smell so delicious I have to stifle a groan.

With a quick glance down the hallway and back, I leave my shit outside my door and follow the direction of the blur toward the shrill screech of the alarm, the scent of sugar and vanilla getting stronger. I hop up on a chair, not caring that I know nothing about this person, or that I just stepped my dirty boot on their frilly chair and hit the button on the fire alarm. And as silence descends, I turn back toward the door. It's to everyone's benefit if I just keep my thoughts to myself and get out of here. For fuck's sake, I don't have anything nice to say right now.

The door clicks closed behind me, and I do a quick dig in my duffle for my key, finding it as the elevator door slides open. I nod to the guy flipping through a keyring as he saunters in my direction, or more accurately, toward the apartment next door to me. I shake my head and step through my door, dragging my bags and rucksack inside.

Before the door fully closes, I let a dig that I'm not proud of slide out of my mouth.

Just loud enough to be heard as the door next to mine opens.

"Fucking New Yorkers."

Lyla

"What did you say?" I ask, spinning to face Josh, my favorite maintenance man of the building. If he didn't have a girlfriend, I'd ask him out. But alas, my luck in love runs pretty solidly toward crappy.

Josh pauses in the hall outside my kitchen messing with the smoke detector that I swear on all things good and holy has a mind of its own. Or maybe the thing is possessed. I don't know.

"Wasn't me," he says, clicking the cover back in place

on the stupid noisemaker. "Did you turn this off yourself?"

"*Pfft.* As if. You know I can't reach that high. I thought you turned it off, and why didn't you just use your key? I could've had an actual fire in here running to the door to let you in." I prop my hands on my hips and wait for a response.

"Lyla, I did," he huffs. "I took me a minute to get up here."

"You didn't knock, follow me in and work your magic to turn that thing off?" I ask, pushing my bangs away from my face with the back of my hand.

"Nope. I'd have used my key like I do every single time you bake." Josh glances at me and then goes back to staring down my unofficial kitchen timer. If only it were accurate.

"Hmmm. Maybe it's fixed?" I doubt it. Honestly, I'm starting to lean more toward the theory that the thing is possessed.

I lead Josh into the kitchen and fold a box from my shop, *Bonne Chatte et Patisserie*, transferring four of the vanilla crème brûlée into it. Tying the box with red and white string, I hand him goodies.

"Thank you. I'm so sorry. I probably took you away from dinner or something with Eva. The least I can do is provide dessert for you guys," I chirp. "But I need feedback on it. I changed things up a little and would love to hear what you think."

"Something," Josh mumbles. "Definitely something."

It takes me a moment to catch on to just what he's saying, or *not* saying as the case may be. And then, I cringe. With my face hidden in my hands, I repeat my apology over and over until Josh interrupts me.

"Forget it. But hey, your new neighbor is here. I saw him go into his apartment when I got off the elevator."

"Next door? You said *him*? Is he old? He's probably old, right?" I shoot my questions at him, rapid-fire.

Josh turns toward the door and answers my questions the same way I asked them, "Yes. Yep. Nope. Not at all." He steps out into the hallway and lifts the pastry box in thanks as he hurries to the elevator.

I lean out the door and say, "Tell Eva I'm so, *so* sorry."

The door next to me swings open, and a giant of lean muscle, scruffy cheeks, and deep, dark brown scowling eyes steps out into the hallway, startling me.

With a really unladylike gasp, I stumble backward until my back hits the doorjamb. "Oh, I'm so sorry," I squeak. "You scared me. Welcome. Kent emailed me that he'd sublet his place for a couple of months, though he didn't tell me anything about you. Not that he needed to. I mean, it's none of my business, really. I'm Lyla Dupree. It's lovely to meet you." I thrust my hand out to shake, but he just stares, so I let it fall back to my side.

I'm rambling, and I can't seem to stop. It's my thing

when I'm nervous, but my roommate, Sasha, tells me it comes off as bubbly and kind of sweet. From the look on this guy's face, though, I wonder if she's just been blowing sunshine up my butt because he looks pissed. And that just makes me even more nervous, so the bubbly word vomit continues.

"You picked an amazing place to live while you're here in the city. Where are you from? Somewhere out west, maybe? I mean, not that I know. I already told you that Kent didn't give me any deets, so it's just a guess, but with the flannel and the beanie..." *Dear Jesus, now would be a perfect time for me to shut up.*

"Anyway, I just finished testing a new recipe. I'm a chef. I don't know if Kent mentioned that when you talked about the sublet, but he should have. I mean, I do pastries, and my roommate does more of the real food. Oh my God, she makes the best mac and cheese, oh and grilled cheese. You'd think that's something anyone can do, but she's a savant with it. Truly, she's amazing. Kent said it was a good thing he had to leave for this assignment in London. Something about gaining weight if he lived next to us for too much longer. I don't know, though. I think something might have happened between him and Sasha, you know? They both kind of started acting funny, and then the next thing I know he's taking a job in England for a year. But, whatever. Do you like sweets? Cakes, cookies, pastries? Any food allergies I should know about?"

And, cue uncomfortable silence.

Absolute utter silence as he stares at me with his brows pinched together and—yeah, the look on his face is one of disgust. I obviously overdid it with the rambling and the rapid-fire, speed-dating type questions.

I glance to the hand, resting on his left hip. No ring, not that it matters. Shifting my weight to my other foot—closer to him—I take a deep breath and blow it out, apologizing once again. "I'm sorry"—I offer my hand, again, smiling big—"I'm your new neighbor. Welcome home."

"You need to fix your smoke alarm," he grumbles. And then he turns and walks away. Hands shoved in the pockets of his coat, he's all broad shoulders and broody. His ass is a work of art leading to muscular thighs perfectly encased in denim. The way he moves is all confidence and a healthy side of *don't mess with me*, almost like he's pissed off at the world.

He steps onto the elevator without a backward glance, a man on a mission. And that thought makes me wonder just what it would be like to be his mission. It's been way too long since the last time… I shake my head, trying to clear the muzzy haze that seems to have settled in my brain while watching the bunch and shift of his muscles as he walked away from me.

He.

Him.

It strikes me that he didn't introduce himself. Didn't even shake my hand, nothing. Thoughts of my mystery neighbor tumble around in my head as I go back into the kitchen and clean up my mess.

Washing dishes is usually pretty therapeutic for me, but tonight, it's just not cutting it. I'm antsy, and my brain is working overtime. A quick glance at the clock on the stove unfortunately shows that I've got hours until Sasha's home from work. I either need to talk it out or bake the jitteriness away.

I pull my bowls back out of the cupboard and start assembling the dough for *kouign amann*. I roll the name of the croissant-like pastry around in my mind as I mix—and fold and roll and fold again—stretching the dough as I stretch out the syllables.

My overactive brain calms as the attention to detail required for this fussy pastry takes front and center. And the fact that it cooks at a low temperature is a bonus. Setting off the alarm twice in one night would just be bad form.

For the most part, the residents on this floor let the whole alarm thing slide. I tend to smooth things over with sweet treats on a regular basis, but I don't want to push my luck tonight.

I lose myself in the process, and when the layered rounds of buttery cakes are tucked safely in the oven, baking low and slow, I clean up again. Then, I pour myself a glass of wine—not a proper pour but a college-girl pour, filling the glass to the rim—and settle into my cozy corner of the couch. I pick up my Kindle and sip my wine as I wait for the timer—the actual timer, not the smoke alarm—to tick down to zero. When the delicious scent of butter wafts through the room, I shuffle to the kitchen and peek at the progress, making sure the dough is puffing up and the layers are forming nicely.

I top off my wine and slide the baking sheets from the oven as a key scrapes in the lock, and the apartment door opens.

Sasha stops short at the entry to the kitchen, and her eyes bounce from the open oven to the sensitive alarm, finally landing on me. "How many times did it blare today?" she asks, dropping her bag to the floor by the closet. She unwinds her scarf and peels off her coat, kicking her shoes under the chair in our entryway. "And what the hell happened to your chair?"

I toss the towel I used as a hot pad over my shoulder and peek around her. Sure enough, there's a big, dirty boot print on the slipcover. "I don't know."

Sasha hits me with a look that calls bullshit and pours the rest of the bottle of wine into a fresh glass.

"Ass. The alarm went off once—only once—and I seriously don't know how it got turned off." I explain the knocking on the door and Josh showing up after the fact. "But the chair is a complete mystery."

"So you made *kouign amann*," she says, nodding at the fresh pastries on the counter, purposely doing away with the French accent, so it sounds more like *queen a-man*. Sasha takes a delicate sip of her wine, swirling, sniffing and tasting it like a pro.

"I did. Sue me. I'm a stress baker." I shrug. "Besides, I should probably bring some to the new guy in Kent's apartment. He seems kinda grumpy."

"You met him? Jesus, was the alarm going off? Does he know what he's in for, living next door to Lyla-bakes-a-lot?" She whips her head around to stare at me, eyes wide, brows high. "Lyla," she says, realization stretching out my name.

I hum a very innocent "Mmmm…?" around my wine goblet.

She knows me far too well. We studied together at the Culinary Institute of America, upstate from here, and we've been friends ever since. When she decided to make the move to the city, it only made sense for us to be roommates. So, there's not much I can hide from her, and even on a good day, I sure as hell can't lie to save my life. I just don't have it in me.

"You nervous rambled, didn't you? How much did you tell him? Oh, dear God, did you ask him about food allergies?" She sets her wine glass on the counter and stares at me. Hard.

I grin awkwardly. There's no need to verbally respond.

She knows I asked.

Of course, I asked.

"It would be irresponsible not to," I tell her. And then I promptly choke on big a gulp of wine, coughing and sputtering until I catch my breath.

Sasha opens the fridge and rifles through it, finding nothing that doesn't require preparation. The last thing she ever feels like is throwing together food for herself after getting home from working the dinner shift. "I can't believe you. So, what's his name?"

Here we go.

"I don't know." She gives me *that* look again, so I walk through to the living room and plop back down on the couch. "I don't. I introduced myself and may or may not have rambled a bit—I'm not confirming that—and he just stood there staring at me. Honestly, it was kind of rude." I shrug, and bite my lower lip, trying hard to fight my smile.

"What's with the face?" Sasha asks, following me.

I shake my head and wave my hand dismissively, hoping she'll drop it.

She won't.

"He's hot, isn't he?" If she cocks her hip any further to the side, she just might throw her back out. "Tell me he's not all hipster artsy with the flannel and the skinny jeans rolled up. The perfectly groomed beard and a messenger bag—please say it ain't so. That's the mess you fall for all the time, and shockingly, it never works out for you."

She's not wrong. That's exactly the boy I followed east from Denver. And exactly the type to have dropped me like a fallen soufflé—just like my mother said would happen. But this one?

Flannel? Check.

Jeans? Not skinny, but perfectly filled out.

Beard?

"It's more scruff than a beard, and believe me, there is nothing hipster or artsy about this guy. He screams grumpy, grumbly mountain man," I say wistfully. I've been on the east coast for over a decade, but I can still spot the real deal without batting an eye.

"Oh, boy," she mumbles under her breath.

"What?"

"That look can only mean one thing." Sasha finishes her wine and continues, "He reminds you of home. You're going to go back to Colorado and leave me, aren't you?"

And prove my mother right?

"Not a chance."

Three

Raleigh

I jump from my bed and promptly fall flat on my face. Well, almost on my face. I manage to catch myself as I go, landing and rolling until I'm well and truly fucked, sheets tangled around my legs.

Why? Because that fucking alarm is blaring again at —Jesus, it's barely four-thirty in the morning. Who the hell gets up this early?

I lie on the floor, waiting for silence to break through the wailing—and I wait. And wait some more. Obviously, it's not happening for me, so I kick my way free and pull on a t-shirt and a pair of sweatpants.

With the heel of my hand, I pound on the wall

between my apartment and the one next door—like that's going to make a difference. I'm sure the curvy little baker can't hear anything over that obnoxious noise.

I open my door, expecting to see something, but there's not a soul out there. Do these people not even react to a smoke alarm anymore? Is this so commonplace that they ignore it? Talk about a modern-day *boy-who-cried-wolf* situation.

I knock loudly on the door, rattling it in its frame, but there's no response. Of course, there's not.

I do it again with one hand on the wall between our doors, the other poised, ready to rain down all my frustration and fury, when the door flies open. And just like yesterday, the blur of curves and wild golden hair scurries away, talking the entire time.

The fuck is wrong with this chick? She lives in this city filled with murderers and crime, and doesn't even bother to check who she's opening the door to? Just lets any schmuck walk in and shut off her alarm?

Like yesterday, I step up on the chair and kill the alarm, thumping back down to the floor as a gasp pauses me from bolting.

"Oh my God, you scared the crap out of me," the chick says. *What did she say her name was? Lily? Liza?* Her eyes widen as I shift, turning to fully face her.

"Listen…"

"Lyla. It's Lyla, and you are?" She thrusts her hand out to shake.

Because I was just ripped from my bed, and I'm admittedly tired and cranky as fuck, I stare at it for a full thirty seconds before reaching out to take it. Her hand is soft and warm, and it practically disappears within my own. And the crazy thing: she gasps again. Quietly this time, but I can feel her holding her breath.

"Raleigh Jacobs. This has to stop, though," I tell her.

Lyla bites her lip and exhales, nodding. "I'm so sorry. I don't know what's going on; the maintenance guys don't either. They've looked at it a million times and can't figure out why it keeps going off. It seems to be just my apartment, but…" She takes a step back, pulling her hand from my grasp far too soon. "Stay right there." She scampers off toward the kitchen, returning quickly with something wrapped in a napkin. A smile stretches across her pretty face as she practically shoves the napkin at me. If it weren't too early to function, I might have enjoyed how her smile transforms her face into… *Fuck it.* It is early. Too early to deal with anyone or anything. Too early to be civil, by any means.

"What the hell is this?" I grumble instead.

One eyebrow pops up, and her free hand settles on her hip, drawing my attention to some gorgeous curves. Her sunny smile turns cloudy. "It's an apology in the form of a chocolate croissant."

Pffft. I huff out a sardonic laugh. "I don't eat that sugary shit," I say, stalking to the door. I turn back just as I step through to the hallway. "Just stop burning crap and keep the alarm from waking up the world."

I watch her hand fall to her side as the door slams shut behind me. And that—the fucking door banging closed—is what pulls curious heads from a handful of apartments up and down the hall, faces glaring at me.

Me.

This chick practically burns down the building on a regular basis and no one bats an eye. I close a door less than delicately and get the death glare. Granted, it is early enough to piss me off, and generally speaking, I'm an early riser.

Since I'm up, I get in a quick workout in my living room. I'll look for the building's gym tonight after work. For now, though, it's just some pushups and squats to get my blood moving. Well, it's mostly to tame some fucking aggression and try to center myself. Calm down and get my head straight for what will likely be a sucky day of getting up to speed on this job.

For the record, it doesn't work.

I shower and get dressed, look around for the coffee maker that Kent said was all set up and ready to go with enough caffeine for a good week. All I find is one of those frous-frous, single-serve machines that make weak-ass brown water.

In the bowl of flavored coffee cups, I find a notecard with my name on the front. As I open the note, a business card falls to the counter. I push it aside to decipher the hastily scrawled note:

> *Raleigh, I left a bunch of coffee flavors that I found in the cabinet. But if you want good coffee, use the Frequent Frappe card I put in here. Don't let the name scare you, this place does French press and espresso like nowhere else. Tell Dupree I sent you. She'll hook you up. -Kent*

I pick up the card and check the address and find that it's not more than a couple of blocks from my job site. Hopefully, I can grab something to eat there too. Slinging my rucksack over my shoulder, I lock up and stride toward the elevator, throwing a glare at the apartment next door. You know, for good measure.

What the hell is it with that chick? The way she babbles on and on about nothing. The constant kitchen experiments.

That alarm.

I can't be the only person in the building annoyed by her, can I? If I see Thomas in the lobby tonight, I'll have to remember to ask him about it. Maybe lodge an official complaint.

I step out onto the sidewalk. The crush of disappointment at the stagnant city air is immediate and harsh. I step up to the curb and hail a cab, half hoping it's Roy from yesterday. Four cabs pass me, all with their lights lit up like fare-seeking beacons, almost like an advertisement that they're blowing me off.

Finally, a cab screeches to a stop, and I climb in giving him the address of Kent's coffee place. Hopefully, the place is open early. It has to be, right? I mean, who the hell opens a coffee shop in the city that never sleeps and doesn't open at the ass crack of dawn?

"Thanks," I grunt, stepping out of the cab. I pull the card from my pocket and check the name: *Bonne Chatte et Patisserie.* My French is rusty as shit, but I have to chuckle. Pretty sure it translates into Good Pussy and Bakery or some shit.

I can't imagine that this fussy pastry shop is going to blow my mind on coffee, but at least I'll be able to grab something to eat.

The door opens, filling the air with the warm aroma of strong coffee and something sweet and delicious. The scent of sugar mixes with vanilla and cinnamon. Normally, the chocolate undercurrent would put a big, old smile on my face, but after this morning's encounter —and last night's too—I need to steer clear of that particular flavor.

The line moves quickly for how packed the place is. The barista must be running like a bat out of hell to keep up the pace. Or the coffee is just that good and has her wired.

"What can I get you?" the rail-thin chick behind the counter asks. She seriously doesn't stop moving— crafting beverages, boxing up croissants and muffins and more, all while barking out names.

I wait for her to pause, and when she does, I realize, once again, I'm not in my laid-back coffee shop at home.

"You need a minute. Step aside dude." She pushes the bangs of her short black hair back off her forehead.

"Sorry. No, I'm ready. I was just—"

"What do you want?" She enunciates each word, speaking slowly and louder than strictly necessary, like I'm a foreigner. And I guess I really am. I don't belong here.

"Sorry."

She hits me with a look, head cocked, brows raised. Expectant and impatient.

"Americano, extra shot and two of those chocolate croissants, please." So much for avoiding.

She taps at her iPad, already pulling pastries from the case. I slide my card to pay and watch, fascinated as she goes through the motions of fixing my drink, all while she nods at the guy behind me spewing his order.

Buttery layers melt in my mouth, meshing with the bittersweet glaze as I sink my teeth into the first crois- sant. I groan at the orgasmic burst of flavors, earning myself another look from the chick behind the counter. Screw her and her judgment—obviously, she's not eating enough of what she's selling.

She drops my brown and black to-go cup on the counter, and it's only then that I remember the rewards card that Kent left for me.

I pull it from my pocket and try to hand it to her. "Hey, sorry. I was told to tell Dupree that Kent sent me." As the words leave my mouth, I realize how stupid I must sound. This place is obviously popular and crazy-busy. Surely, there's more than one Kent in the city. When the angry girl's face turns red and her jaw tics, I can feel the annoyance rolling off of her.

Without missing a beat, she turns and yells over her shoulder, "LD, I got one of Kent's friends out here."

Ready to cut my losses, I say, "Sorry, I'll just come back another time and…" I let the statement fizzle. I've apologized to this kid three times already. I'm well over my quota for this early in the day.

"Punch him and tell him thank you, Sam. You know the drill."

That voice. It's familiar, but that makes no sense. I don't know anyone here. Maybe it's the lack of accent that makes me think I've heard it before. It almost sounds like home.

"Dude, I got a line out the door, and it's freezing out there. Gimme a hand, a'ight?" Then, under her breath,

Sam adds, "And you'd fire my ass if I punched him the way I want."

Great. I find a seriously good hook-up for breakfast close to work, and I've already pissed off the chick in charge of my morning fuel.

The doors to the kitchen swing open as I take a drink and burn the fuck out of not just my tongue, but the back of my throat, where the coffee lodges itself, mid-swallow. Because who walks out, smiling and happy as she can fucking be, but my goddamn alarm-loving neighbor.

"Lyla?" I croak around the third-degree burns. "Why are you here?" *The fuck?*

"Raleigh," she says, her voice dripping with sugary sweetness. "Hand me your card, and I'll get you taken care of." She leans over the counter, a lock of honey blonde hair falling forward out of her bandana. No stuffy chef's hat for this girl. "I'd offer you the pastry du jour, but it's chock full of sugar, so I doubt you'd be interested." Her gaze drops to the half-eaten chocolate croissant in my hand, and a delighted smile pushes her rosy cheeks high on her face.

Busted—bigger than shit—by my neighbor. I choose to ignore the burn in my cheeks, and my bullshit lies from this morning. I don't have to admit to anything.

She slowly takes my card and punches a perfect hole in the shape of a cat through one of the cups printed along the bottom of the card. And then, with a wink, she punches another precise cat through the next two cups and hands the card back across the counter.

"There you go. You enjoy your day, Raleigh," she says full of effervescence. "Come back again."

Shoving the card in my pocket, I lift my cup in a silent salute, keeping my lips sealed. But I do make sure to grab my other croissant off the counter. I'm not a big enough fool to leave that behind for the sake of pride or whatever.

And I make a mental note to look for a new coffee shop before tomorrow.

R aleigh Jacobs blushes when he's embarrassed. I file that little tidbit under *Things I Didn't Know I Needed to Know.* No telling when I'm going to need to pull that fact out of my arsenal.

"Who the hell was that asshole?" Sam asks after the morning rush breaks. It's obvious who she's talking about. Raleigh is the only asshole who stands out from all the others. He's obviously not a New Yorker. He wears it loudly in his rugged appearance, in the way he interacts with people. He's polite and uses very middle of the country manners. At least, he uses them with everyone other than me.

I wipe down my work surface, preparing to start in on the day's special. I have precious few hours to get ready—maybe two, tops—before the next influx of customers.

"Cut him some slack. He's not from here," I tell Sam. My eyes tear as I dice the onions I pulled from the cooler for chicken salad. It's a last-minute decision for lunch today, but it's easy and almost always goes over really well. And I'm drained from scrambling this morning. I didn't anticipate another encounter with Raleigh on my way out the door.

"How do you know?" Sam grabs the chicken breasts that I somehow managed to poach this morning between rotating muffins and other treats in and out of the ovens.

She can be a bit brusque at times, but there aren't many twenty-somethings I've met who have the work ethic and desire to learn that she does. I lucked out the day she walked into my shop, cold and hungry. Nothing like being down on your luck and grateful for a hand up.

I blow at the stupid piece of hair that keeps falling out of my bandana, hoping it stays out of my eyes for more than a minute or two.

"He's my new neighbor, and we, uh…" I tilt my head from side to side, thinking. Sam's been with me long enough that she knows all about the stupid smoke alarm in my apartment. "We've had a couple of run-ins already. He's why I was running a little late this morning."

I take a deep breath through my mouth and plant my tongue on the roof of my mouth. I don't care how many thousands of pounds of onions I've chopped over the years, I will never, ever not tear up. I've tried every trick in the book—even swim goggles—but nothing works for me. I'm an onion crier.

"He made you late?" she asks, eyebrows popping. "Didn't seem like he was all that happy to see you, so I'm guessing you weren't bumping uglies." There's no break, not even a stutter in the rhythmic *chop chop chop* of her knife against the cutting board as she tosses that out there.

Lips pursed, I shake my head. "Far from it, and… really? That's what we're calling it now?" Overall, the stuff she says doesn't shock me anymore, but every now and then, I like to get her to check herself. At least, I try to.

She pauses and looks across the prep table. "What? Those parts aren't all that pretty to look at. Have you ever watched porn?"

I drop my knife to the cutting board and plop my head into my hands. Jesus, maybe she *can* still shock me.

Without missing a beat, Sam takes in my teary eyes and nods at my oniony hand right next to them. "Make sure you wash your hands before you pick that knife up again."

I don't know how many times I said those very

words in the first month or two, while I trained her. It's funny hearing them tossed back at me. And I would love to point out the fact that she glossed right past her comment about porn. Or maybe I should just be relieved that she did. I scrub my hands and go to the storage shelves, pulling down walnuts and dried cranberries.

"So, the porn. Yes or no? And you haven't weighed in yet, on whether you were bumping with him. Personally, I don't swing that way, but it looked like he filled out his jeans pretty well. Front and back."

The bags I'm carrying hit the counter with a thump, followed closely by my forehead.

My words are muffled since I'm basically talking to a block of wood—in more ways than just the most obvious. "Sam, stop. Do you even listen to the things that come out of your mouth?" I lift my head and wipe the counter clean, catching her saucy look. "No, I'm not sleeping with him. I just met him last night. He's had the full fire alarm experience twice already, and that includes first thing this morning. He pounded on my door, pissed off, and ripped me a new one, thus making me late."

She stares at me for a full minute before she shrugs with a *huh*. "Did you offer him some pastries? You wouldn't believe the sound he made when he bit into your chocolate croissant. It was like pure sex spilling from his lips. I mean, his eyes rolled back and everything. Again, if I liked dudes, I'd have signed up for *his* rewards program. Know what I mean?"

Holy hell, she's killing me. I pull the huge mixing bowl out and start adding the diced chicken and onions, cranberries, and chopped nuts. I combine the ingredients, season everything, and pull fresh mayonnaise from the fridge, opting not to address her comment.

"Nothing? I get nothing from you now?" Sam starts in on prepping romaine for the salad. "You gonna try to tell me that dude's not hot? A little older maybe, but that probably just means he's had practice, knows what he's doing with what he's packing."

My head whips up and I stare at her, finally well and truly shocked by what's coming out of her mouth.

"Because let me be clear here, Lyla. That man is packing."

"You're fired." It's the only thing I can say. She knows I'm not serious. I've been training her to run this place for far too long, but honestly, I don't even know with her anymore. "Why don't you go check the fruit salad up front? And the chips. I just..." I wave my hands at her and let the sentence die because I don't know what to say. And he can't be but a few years older than me, right?

"I'll give you a minute because I know that's what you're really asking for. But Lyla, you need to break your streak. Use it or lose it, that shit's getting cobwebby down there."

I stop folding in the mayo and stare blankly at her.

She blows out a gusty laugh. "Dude, you need to get laid."

With that, Sam goes back out front, giving me the illusion of peace and a whole lot to think about.

The rest of the day passes in a blur. The kind of blur that keeps me in business, pays the bills, and makes my dreams come true.

Thank God.

I've worked my ass off to make my little piece of Manhattan a sought-after success, and I can finally breathe easy enough to think hard about expansion. A new location. Where to do it is the real problem, though. My advisor has run the numbers, and while Minneapolis and Kansas City both have good markets, the Denver numbers look best. It just feels wrong to go home and face my mother with her resounding proclamation that I never should have followed *that boy* to New York.

It's true, I shouldn't have, but I don't need her to rub it in my face.

Now, though, is the time of day I love the best. Or second best, because creating the food, the pastries, and seeing the enjoyment of those things plastered across the faces of my customers is truly my favorite thing ever. But at the end of every day, when I close my doors for the afternoon, I'm all alone with nothing but my thoughts and inspirations, and usually a glass of wine.

Sam might be gone for the day, but her words buzz loudly around my brain, which is silly. I mean it's not like I didn't notice Raleigh and his hotness. There's no way I could miss it.

It sure didn't escape observation, the way his shoulders tested the seams of his gray Avalanche t-shirt when I opened my door to him this morning. And I certainly didn't miss the black joggers he was wearing.

New Yorkers are loyal to their sports teams, even though they're pretty divided within a given sport with multiple teams in the same city. But Denver fans tend to put the fan in fanatical. That might just make Raleigh Jacobs a fellow Coloradan.

It's not like I didn't get that vibe from him already. The rugged look, scruff, flannel, and work boots that look like they've seen some miles. The ever-present beanie. And his apparent dislike for the Big Apple—that alone is telling if nothing else.

I'd put my money on those muscles he's sporting being organically grown. Hiking, skiing, chopping wood —God, help me, the thought of watching that man swing an axe. *Mmm.* The mere possibility makes me long for home in a way that I haven't in ages. If only it were that simple.

I pour myself an extra hefty glass of wine and do a thorough cleaning of my kitchen, checking stock and jotting down things I need to place an order for. I carry my cleaning frenzy through to the front of the shop and, out of nowhere, I picture Raleigh clutching a half-eaten *pain au chocolat,* with a smudge of chocolate clinging to his bottom lip. What I wouldn't give to lick it clean.

And, since he obviously lied earlier, why did he refuse my peace offerings in my apartment? I don't know whether I should take that rejection to heart or if he was just being the grumpy-ass I think he might be. He obviously doesn't hate that sugary shit quite the way he proclaimed first thing this morning.

Maybe he was just cranky from sleeping in a strange place. And maybe it was the stupid alarm. I can't blame him there. It pisses me off all the freaking time, and I've come to expect it.

More than anything, I think maybe he just needs a friend. This city can be a lonely place, hard to navigate if you're all alone.

With as much as Sasha and I work—the hours we put in—it would be tough to make friends here if we didn't already have a solid base. As it is, working very opposite hours from her, I'm lonely.

I'm lonely.

The realization hits me like an epiphany, and I still, mid-swipe of my broom. I like my life here in New York—the hustle and bustle, the opportunities for culture in the city. But I'm really pretty sequestered, at least in the important ways. My love life is nonexistent, and the only people I interact with on a regular basis are Sam, Sasha, and her friends. And the maintenance guys in my building. Each of those relationships exists in very well-defined parameters and separate from the others.

Maybe I need a change, a little project to throw myself into.

Maybe *I* need a new friend.

I stare out the front window, crisp white snow lightly falling in the fading light of the day. It's beautiful. But only because the sidewalk, where it turns to brown and then black sludge, is hidden from my view.

Life is all about perspective.

The snow twinkles magically against the lights of the city skyline, but on the ground, it's a filthy nuisance. New York has endless opportunities for things to do, things to see, but sometimes, it can feel soiled and overwhelming. There are millions of people here. And, yet, it can feel like the loneliest place on earth.

Yeah, something needs to change.

I finish sweeping and give the floor a hasty mop. Quickly assembling what I need for tomorrow, I decide to come in early in the morning to get a jump on things, as opposed to staying any later. I did okay winging lunch today; tomorrow's offerings will be just as good, if not better.

Tonight, I need to go home, have some wine and cheese for dinner, and make a plan. Figure out how to transform my new neighbor into my new friend.

Five

Raleigh

My phone rings as soon as I clear the stairs to street level. I hate the fucking subway. I spent most of my day down in those filthy tunnels, like a mole. Or a rat. At least it's warm down there.

Wind whips down the avenue, funneled between tall buildings, rushing over the black slush and chilling the night air even more. I pull my phone from my pocket to see who's calling, even though I hate taking calls on the sidewalk.

Laney's name might be lit up on the screen, but it's a

picture of Matty's toothless grin that greets me. It's still a toss-up who's calling, but no matter how much I dread the idea of speaking to the wicked witch, I take the call. I don't want to miss out on the opportunity to talk to my little guy.

"Hey, just give me a minute," I say, picking up my pace toward the sanctuary of my building. I push through the doors and practically collide with one of the other residents. I give him a chin lift and mouth sorry as I make my way to the elevators.

In the month I've been here, all I've done is work, sleep, visit Matty a couple of times, and build my immunity to the sound of smoke alarms. I'm pretty sure that last one could be a safety issue.

"Okay, I'm inside, but I might lose you in the elevator. What's up?" I ask, assuming it's my ex-wife who's calling.

"Dad. Where are you? Did you go to the zoo yet? Did you see the dinos at the museum? Are you coming home to see me this weekend? I miss you. Mom says you're not home enough, and she needs a break."

And I would be wrong.

"Hey, Matty. Slow down, bud. How are you? How was school today?" I ask, finding myself stacking questions much like he just did.

He sighs dramatically. "It was okay, I guess. So are you coming home? Daddy, please?"

I wish I could.

"Sorry, buddy, not this weekend. Remember on our hike last visit? I told you we'd have to wait a little bit. We looked at the calendar and put a green line around the next time I come home."

I want to make it easy for him to track the time between visits, to mark the passing of time.

"Yeah." His voice wobbles like it does when he's trying not to get caught for spilling milk.

"And when all the squares are colored in, then you know I'm coming home, right?" I was actually pretty proud of myself for thinking of this. Each day, Matty gets to fill in the grid square, effectively counting down the days between visits.

"But Dad, they *are* all colored in, so that means you can come home now," he says, excitement bouncing through the phone.

"Matt. That's not how this works, bud. One a day— we talked about this."

It kills me not seeing my son every day.

Not being there to talk about his day.

Not being there for the never-ending adjustment to having your parents split up.

Not being there to hug on him and tell him every-thing's going to be okay.

Silence turns to sniffles, and I thank the cellular gods that the call didn't drop between the lobby and my floor.

My kid needs me. I stride down the hall and am just pushing through my door when it happens.

The fucking alarm.

"Dad?" Matty shrieks, full of panic and tears. "Mom, Daddy's in a fire. What if he dies? Daddy… Daddy…" he wails, drowning me out when I call to him.

My heart fucking breaks hearing my kid think the worst.

I pound on Lyla's door and, thankfully, she opens it quickly.

"I'm sorry. I—"

I don't give her a chance to finish whatever excuse she's about to sling. Instead, I push into her foyer and step up onto the chair, silencing the alarm.

"Matty. Matthew," I shout into the phone. "I'm fine. Listen to me buddy, the alarm is off. It's gone. Come on dude, you need to calm down and listen to my voice."

The sounds of his terror fade and are replaced with Laney telling him to go to his room and get it together.

"Why, Raleigh? Now you have to scare the shit out of him over the phone? Do you have any idea what my night is going to look like now? He's already hard to deal with, talking about you all the time, and always asking when you're coming home. Jesus, how long is it until bedtime?" Cabinet doors slam in the background, followed by the beep of buttons on the microwave.

Was Laney always this bad?

Without a backward glance, I stalk out of Lyla's door and through mine, letting it slam hard behind me. *How much worse can this day get?*

"Don't. I'd trade places with you in a heartbeat, you know that. I'd give my left nut to spend this evening with Matty, and you sure as fuck know I didn't scare him intentionally," I tell my ex-wife, glaring at the wall separating me from Lyla and her fucking alarm.

I wish the conversation could improve from here, but that would be hoping for too much. The only good thing is when Laney finally concedes to letting Matty get back on the phone, so I can assure him that I'm alright. That I'm safe, and that I'll see him next Friday. I promise to talk to him every day and do the countdown that way until I'm home again.

After a teary good-bye, I drop my phone to the counter and shed my jacket and boots, getting comfortable. Guess I'm ordering in tonight because there's nothing here to cook, and I don't have it in me to go out and deal with any more people—hell, with the city in general—tonight.

I pop the lid off a beer as a tentative knock sounds at the door. Opening it, I mentally kick myself for even wondering about things getting worse or not.

It's Lyla.

"What?" I don't have the fucks to give about whether I'm being a dick to her.

And I am.

Being a dick.

She's standing in front of me in maroon leggings that cling to the curve of her thighs, and a hockey jersey. Not just any jersey, but my team's. Denver colors.

"Raleigh, I'm really sorry. That was obviously worse timing than usual"—I hit her with a glare, and her cheeks pink up—"not that there's ever a good time. But I swear, the maintenance guys are up here all the time trying to put an end to the mayhem. My apartment hates me. It's a fact, but I brought you dinner to celebrate your first month in the city. You're going to have to eat it quickly though, because I decided it was time for you to get out and do something fun.

"All you do is sleep, work, and travel. So I took a chance, a wild guess. I mean, I might be wrong, but I think I nailed it, so get your shoes back on and grab your coat. I have some to-go cups, so actually we can scoop your dinner into one of those, and you can eat on the way. People eat on the subway all the time. It's weird and takes some getting used to when you first get here, but it's just part of the experience. Okay, so we have to bolt pretty quick. I'll run and grab one of those cups, maybe two. You don't care if I have some too, do you?"

I have no idea what's happening, what she's talking

about. I'm not sure she's taken a breath since I opened the door, but the words just tumbled out of her mouth the entire time she buzzed around my kitchen, fussing with the casserole dish she brought. Throwing away the cap from my beer bottle. Wiping the already clean counters—I haven't cooked here, so it's not like they're dirty.

Her smile is a little unsure as she pauses halfway out my door, but her eyes are dancing. Sparkling excitedly. And then she bites her damn lip. She does that a lot after doing her word vomit thing, like she knows she just let it get away from her.

It's adorable. Like her.

"Okay, I'll be right back," she says, shimmying a little on the balls of her feet. And while that move is cute, the way it makes her breasts bounce isn't cute at all. No, it's something entirely different, and I kind of want to see her do it again, enjoy the show now that I know the magic of watching her move. But Lyla turns on her heel and heads out my door, flipping the deadbolt so she can pop right back in. With to-go cups? *Is that what she said?*

My stomach growls, pulling me from the trance Lyla's babbling tends to put me in. I lift a corner of the foil covering the baking dish she set on the stove. Steam swirls the scent of buttery cheese and pasta, Cajun spices, and meat all around me. It smells delicious, and I pop a bit into my mouth, groaning as the flavors burst on my tongue.

I look over my shoulder at the small sound of a gasp. Lyla's standing in my entryway, cardboard cups clutched to the front of her puffy coat. Purse slung across her chest. Her pretty bow lips parted just enough to let that sound out.

"Sorry," she apologizes, shifting from one foot to the other.

I lick my thumb and raise an eyebrow at her. "What's going on here?" I ask, waving my hand between the food and her.

She drives me crazy, annoys the shit out of me, but she's fucking adorable, and she's staring at my mouth. Hard.

Lyla blinks twice and shakes off whatever thoughts she had swirling through her head.

"I, uh, thought maybe you needed to do something fun for a change. A night out in the city. I made you dinner. Well, us, really"—she's doing it again, the rambling, babbling word vomit—"And we have a player in the building, so I asked if he could hook me up with tickets. I mean, not for free or anything, but I offered him pastries or food to, you know, just to help me get seats in the good section—the fun one—because I know there's a super fun one, but I don't remember the section number. And he just gave me two. For free. I'm going to have to find out what his favorite treats are, though I might wait until after the season is done. I think players eat pretty healthy during the season…"

She finally takes a breath and meets my eye.

"But what are you talking about?" I take the cups from her and grab a spoon, scooping gooey mac and cheese into each of them. I hand her a plastic spoon and dig in, waiting for her to answer. With as much as she talks, I should be able to finish a good chunk of this before she finally gets to the fucking point.

"I… I thought you might be a hockey fan—Denver, specifically." That gets my attention. "I got us tickets to the game tonight. Puck drop is—"

"At seven-thirty."

"Yeah."

I glance at the clock and then back to her. "Do we even have time to get there?" I have no concept of how long it takes to get anywhere other than the airport, the job site and her coffee shop.

Lyla nods. "Yep. But we need to go soon. Now, actually." She grimaces a little, glancing at my boots, my coat, and back to me. "I don't mean to rush you, and geez, I probably should have checked with you first to see if you already had plans tonight or even wanted to go, but once I had the idea, I just got so excited. And I thought maybe it would make up a little bit for the alarm going off all the time. I really am sorry about that. And then you looked so mad, so much more upset this time"—deep breath—"I'm sorry."

"Thank you," I say, sliding my feet into my boots.

"It's just—"

"It's cool." I throw on my coat and beanie, patting my pockets to make sure my gloves are in there. I grab my cup of food and open the door, letting Lyla out. "It was a shit day, but this helps. Thank you."

F ood and hockey seem to have tamed the wild beast.

I add new items to my ever-growing mental file of *Things I Didn't Know I Needed to Know* about Raleigh Jacobs.

Likes comfort foods.

Secretly likes cookies and cakes, truffles, and eclairs.

Freaking loves Colorado hockey.

Thank God for that one. If he were a baseball fan, there's no way I'd have been able to get the stellar tickets I did, let alone sit through an entire game, no matter how much I wanted to show him a good time. *Not like that.*

Though… maybe.

Because fun fact numero four in the mental file from last night's entry is that Raleigh Jacobs is a dad. He shared with me at the game that he'd been on the phone with his son when he got home. Knowing that my alarm scared that little boy, that he thought something bad had happened to his dad, makes me feel worse than ever.

But the way Raleigh's face lit up and his eyes danced when he talked about his son, Matty, made my stupid heart leap with joy.

Damn it.

It's not that I have a problem with any of those things —far from it. But history tends to repeat itself and, that being the case, any pitter-pattering my heart does is just setting the poor thing up to fall.

And not in a good way.

Guys don't like me. Well, they like me—who wouldn't? I'm an amazing friend. They just don't *like* me. I'm not love potential. I guess I just don't have staying power. Sasha calls bullshit on that, but the facts are the facts, and much as it kills me to admit, my mother might have been right. I could practically hear her, *I told you this would happen,* when the boy I moved to New York with dropped me without a backward glance.

So, I did what I had to; pulled myself up, baked myself happy, and absolutely excelled in my culinary program.

I've worked my ass off—not literally though—to get where I am, to have my own successful patisserie. I also have hips and curves. Boobs and booty. I joke that those are all requirements for being a good pastry chef.

While my mom tends toward gaslighting me with her incessant, *I'm just saying, I don't mean to be mean*, Sasha and her friend, Ian, insist that I just haven't found the right person, one who appreciates my ambitions and my curves. But it's all good. I'm happy and successful, and I'm sure as hell not willing to stop enjoying the good things in life.

Love will happen when the time is right. In the meantime, I'll help Raleigh discover the best parts of the city and enjoy his time here.

Sam slides a *cafe au lait* across the butcher block to me, pulling me from my thoughts. "You daydreaming about the D?" she asks, stirring today's soup and ladling a tasting bowl for herself. She nods at the coffee she just delivered and adds, "You look like you could use that."

"Thanks. I think."

"So, the D? You get some yet?" Sam asks between loud and obnoxious slurps of bisque.

"Why are you so invested in my love life? Have I been terrible?" It's entirely possible, I guess.

"Nah, just looking out for your lady bits." *Slurp.* "It's been a while." *Slurp.* "And you have that hot dude that comes in every morning living within arm's reach." *Slurp.* "Just connecting the dots." *Sluuuurrrrp.*

"Would you stop with the noise? You're driving me insane." I take a delicate, perfectly quiet sip my coffee and nibble on a chunk of brie from my cheese plate.

Sam finishes her soup, carefully and quietly, for the most part. She washes her bowl and checks the baguettes, pushing through the swinging doors to the front of the shop. And it hits me.

"What do you mean, he comes in here every morning? Who does? Raleigh?" I follow her out front, cradling my *au lait* mug in my palms. It's mostly empty out here, but I don't need to be yelling from the kitchen.

"Yeah. The dude with the package," she says, her hands cupped in front of her jeans. I scan the customers perched at tables, seeing they both have earbuds in while she continues like it's just the two of us. "You said he was your neighbor that first time he came in. Still don't get why he didn't know how to order his shit and step aside."

She will not let that go. Sam is a New Yorker through and through. Honestly, I'm not sure she's ever been off the island, through a tunnel or over a bridge.

"Every morning?"

How can that be? He's never mentioned it, and I haven't seen his name on any of the full rewards cards turned in. If he's that much of a loyal customer, you'd think he'd want the email of the week's offerings. Or a chance to win the monthly freebie drawing.

"Yep. Without fail. And for what it's worth, he does as good of a service to his khakis as he does his jeans." She blows out a big puff of air and mumbles, "Almost makes a girl think about switching teams."

"But—"

She cuts me off, waving her finger in my face to make her point. "You need to tap that, LD. Seriously."

I don't bother responding. What she's saying doesn't make any sense, and it really doesn't even matter. He's annoyed with me more often than not. We've made some progress into the friend zone, but, again, facts: He's definitely *not* interested. I shake my head and go back to the kitchen. I have numbers to run and location decisions to make. Food to prepare.

No matter how busy the lunch rush gets, I can't seem to shake Raleigh from my thoughts. Obviously, we do good coffee here—amazing, in fact. And he totally lied from day one about not liking sweets, though he still hasn't addressed that head-on. It might be fun to see just how committed he is to maintaining that façade. But the fact that he's been in every single day and I had no idea kind of blows me away.

As my workday winds to a close, I decide to do my

extra baking here for a change. I usually prefer to do my creative test recipes at home, but to be honest, even I'm getting tired of the stupid alarm blaring. So today, I pour myself an extra glass of wine and turn up my music.

Dancing and drinking. Stirring and tasting. The afternoon slides by, leaving me relaxed and happy with boxes upon boxes of tasting samples. Sweets without the noise pollution is just the thing for the residents on my floor.

I make up a special box for Josh and one for Thomas. The maintenance guy and the doorman are both so sweet and good to me, and crazy kinds of patient even though Josh can't seem to figure out the reason for my stupid alarm being so touchy.

As I tie up the boxes, I decide to add a couple extra rich chocolate truffles to the box for Raleigh. Maybe he's not the grumpy asshole he likes to portray himself as. Maybe, just maybe, he's simply missing his kiddo. So, with my arms laden down with bags full of boxes, and boxes full of decadence, I head for home.

With the cold snap this week, I opt for the subway instead of walking the whole way. The platform is full of people, bodies vying for prime access to the trains as they slide into the station.

I'm shaken and jostled, bumped repeatedly, and my toes get stepped on the entire ride uptown, but somehow, I manage to protect my precious cargo. The whipping wind practically blows me down the street and through the revolving door of my building and right into Thomas.

"Let me help you with those, Lyla." He grabs the handles of one bag, but with all the crap I'm toting, and how the bags have gotten twisted around each other, I just about drop everything.

"Nope, I'm good," I insist. I shuffle things a bit and open the bag I need. "Just grab those top couple of boxes for me. Thought I'd give the maintenance guys the night off for a change, so I baked at work and just brought you guys the good stuff. One for you and then one for whoever's on duty tonight. I'll put the others in the maintenance office," I say, blowing back the stupid piece of hair that never seems to want to stay tucked away.

Thomas's face lights up, and I swear he does a little dance in anticipation. "Don't you worry about that. I'll take those back to the office for you since you've got your hands full." He peeks in one of the boxes and winks at me.

"Can I trust you, Thomas? You'll share?"

He's got a mischievous glint in his eye tonight, and he looks like he just might tear through all the sugary goodness himself.

He gathers up the boxes, tucking one next to his phone, and then stalks off down the hall. "I promise," he calls over his shoulder as he walks toward the offices. At least he's making a good show of sharing.

The heavy bags are starting to cut into my arm, so by the time I get to the elevator, I mash the call button and try to shift what I can. The doors open, and I scurry in, hitting seventeen with my elbow. At least I try. I actually got eighteen, but even more surprising is when the car goes down instead of up, opening to the basement level. The horrible, scary basement with the fitness center.

My pointer finger shakes and trembles as I try to do a better job of at least pushing the button for the floor I need. The bags and my purse are heavier than I'm used to.

A hand reaches out, holding the door open, a deep chuckle bouncing off the cinderblock walls.

"You get lost?" Raleigh's deep voice weaves its way through me, sending a little shiver down my spine. He must take pity on me because when he steps into the car, he leans across me and pushes the button for our floor.

I hold my breath, though I'm not sure why. Maybe it's Sam's observations flitting about in my brain, but I just don't move a muscle, instead taking in the scent of fresh sweat and something distinctly him.

I stare at his forearm—*what is it about a man's forearm?*—and blow at the chunk of hair that's flopping down into my face yet again.

"Thanks," I say, clearing my throat. Lord have mercy, are those his thighs? Do normal people have muscles like that?

I probably shouldn't be gawking at his legs and try to force my gaze up to his face, but the journey—oh the journey. Navy gym shorts lead to the sweaty gray t-shirt I love that clings to every bulge and ridge of muscle.

The doors open to the lobby, and it seems as though every single resident in the building is piling into the tight space, forcing me closer to Raleigh than my brain and body could ever be prepared for. He pushes himself deeper into the corner, but as the whacky lady from the tenth-floor digs through her bag, jabbing me with a well-placed elbow, I stumble back, right into him.

He reaches up, steadying me, his hands wrapped around the upper part of my arms.

"Sorry," I say, though Whack-a-doodle just does the hair toss thing that the rest of the world left back in high school. She makes no bones about checking out Raleigh's shoulders, his arms, and most definitely his package.

She doesn't apologize, nor does she acknowledge me at all. She just reaches in her bag, smacking me again, and grabs a business card. She tucks it into Raleigh's hand and tells him, "That's my *personal* cell." She puts her thumb and pinky to the side of her face and mouths *Call me* as she steps off the elevator to her floor.

"What was that?" Raleigh asks.

Almost in unison, everyone left in the car responds with, "Stay clear." Raleigh looks at me with a dark brow raised, and I just shake my head. There's no better explanation beyond that.

At our floor, Raleigh reaches out, parting the remaining bodies to make room for us to exit.

"Thank you," I say, my voice a little stronger this time, and I blow at my loose hair. Having some space between us seems to have reset my brain, allowing me to speak normally again.

Seriously, what happened to me earlier? Must have been the proximity to the treadmills that made me stupid. The lack of altitude? I've never been that close to the building's gym so surely that could make a girl woozy, right?

"No problem. You need a hand with all that?" Raleigh slides his hand around the handles of the bag, and more of those damn sparks send tingles through my body. His stupid t-shirt is stretched to its limits across those shoulders, clinging desperately to the planes of that stupidly muscle-y chest.

I feel myself tipping forward, drawn toward him. I catch myself before it goes too far, though I don't miss the sideways glance from Raleigh as I stutter step to cover whatever that just was. Because I'd rather not think about the why.

"Nope, I've got it. Thanks again"—I reach into my bag and hand him the box I packed especially for him—"I'll just hand the rest of these out down the hall.

Thought I'd give you all an alarm-free treat for a change." I nod, more to myself than Raleigh, and grin what I'm sure is the most awkward baring of teeth, though I'd like to believe it's a bright, happy, sunny smile.

Delusions are evidently my friend at the moment.

Seven

Raleigh

Something's changed. There's been some kind of shift between Lyla and me, but I don't entirely know what to make of it. And I sure as fuck can't put my finger on it.

Though I have been thinking a whole hell of a lot about putting my fingers on her.

My fingers, my hands. My tongue.

Since none of those body parts are going to get to make the switch from fantasy to reality with Lyla, I savor the burst of sweetness and the bite of bitterness perfectly balanced in one of her truffles.

Does she taste half as good?

I shake the thought from my head and dive back into work. Materials shipments have been delayed again; some bureaucratic asshole is out to get me on this project. At every turn, every possible roadblock and detour has happened. I've had guys walk off the job site, materials delays, machinery held up in transit.

It's hell being away from Matty, and the threat of being here any longer than necessary due to all the shit that keeps going sideways just pisses me off.

I miss my kid, and he misses me. It seems like each week gets harder and harder. Every time I go home to spend time with him, it's harder to leave than it was the time before.

The only bright spot that makes this city at all tolerable is my morning coffee and maybe the girl next door. My feelings toward her have dramatically improved since she's been doing her cooking and baking shit at her shop. I just haven't let her in on that little fact. What's the point? I can't have her thinking she's broken through my icy façade.

Jesus, the way she would gloat and bounce around with her hap-hap-happy sunshine would kill me without a doubt.

As it is, I spend way more time than is healthy thinking about her being happy and bouncy.

And how her bouncing could make me so very happy.

We've grabbed dinner a handful of times, and I admit, I've had fun with her—talking, laughing. Then there was that time we were practically pressed into each other in the elevator, her hands full, her cheeks flushed. That stray strand of hair that always seems to fall into her face.

My fingers itched to tuck it back behind her ear. To touch her, feel the flush that heated her cheeks.

I leaned on my doorframe watching her hand out boxes of pastries to everyone on our floor, memorizing the curve of her ass each time she bent to pull another box from the bags at her feet. I had to duck inside when she got to the end of the hall; she sure as fuck didn't need to turn around and see the wood I was sporting. I stood under the coldest shower I could stand before giving in and jerking off to thoughts of her.

I'm a walking contradiction. So much so, that I'm driving myself to drink.

I've been spending a ton of time in the building's gym. It's not nearly as good a workout as hiking or chopping piles of firewood—the shit I usually do—but I need to exorcise my demons somehow.

Tonight, though, I need a break from everything. From the gym. From the cute girl on the other side of my kitchen wall. Most of all, I need a break from pizza, Chinese takeout, and street food.

Due to yet another fucking hang-up, the other engineer on this job and I are heading to Hell's Kitchen. He keeps raving about this little place, Kitchenne, and how the food there is so good, he's proposed to the chef on more than one occasion.

As soon as I walk through the door, I nod to him, where he's set up at the bar. I pull my beanie from my head and run my hand through my hair, taming it as much as I care to. Making my way to the empty seat next to him, I drop my jacket to the back.

"So, this is it?" I look around, taking in the vibe. Thank fuck it's not at all pretentious. The clientele here seems to be a mix of real, every day, run-of-the-mill people.

I do a double take at a couple of guys at the end of the bar closest to the kitchen. The one dude covered in tats and sporting a beanie scowls at his friend, and recognition hits me—he's the drummer from a band that is crushing the alternative music world, The UnBroken. I saw them at Red Rocks over the summer, and their show kicked ass.

"Dude, glad you could make it." John slaps my back and shakes my hand. "You want a beer or something stronger?" he asks, raising his hand to the bartender.

"IPA, please. Something local if you have it," I tell the chick behind the taps as she drops a coaster in front of me. "That's the drummer for The UnBroken down there, isn't it?" I take a pull from my pint and settle into my seat.

John looks past me and nods. "Yeah, I guess. Those guys are here a lot. I thought he looked familiar but couldn't place him." He shrugs and reaches for a menu, telling me about every dish available in ridiculous detail. Dude has it bad for the chef.

I sip my beer, only half-listening to the ramblings of a love-sick fool and enjoy the faint strains of an acoustic set drifting in from the dining room.

"So, what are you getting?" John asks.

Before I can answer him, the door opens, blowing Lyla in on a gust of icy wind. Rosy cheeks, a bright pink slouchy hat on her head, and eyes dancing down the bar —sliding right past me to the guys from the band.

I rub the heel of my palm in the center of my chest and drain the rest of my pint. What the hell is that? Jealousy? I spin the menu and point, no idea what I just ordered. My attention locks in on the curvy blonde at the end of the bar. The one who I was trying to get a little space from. The one who's wrapped up in some other dude's arms.

A fresh beer appears in front of me, and John is talking a mile a minute mostly to the poor bartender. He's waxing poetic about the food here—jockeying for a date with the chef. Pleading his case—when Lyla's room-mate walks out of the kitchen in her white coat and checkered pants, a ball cap with the signature logo for The UnBroken on her head.

Sasha waves to me and when Lyla turns, following her line of sight, our eyes meet. The smile that pushes up her cheeks and lights her entire face does something weird to my chest again. Not quite the same as when she pushed past me down the bar, but… something.

I lift my pint in greeting, wondering when the fuck I lost my man-card and grew a damn vagina.

"That's her. That's the girl I'm stupidly in love with," John says.

I turn back to him, my mouth twisted in a sneer. "She's a pastry chef, you twit. She doesn't work here. Lyla's got her own place down by the job site. And there is no love between the two of you. Not allowed."

"What? Who the hell is Lyla?" He eyes me and then, distracted, continues, "For fuck's sake, I want to peel her out of those checkered pants, and… Do you think she has something lacy on under that white coat?"

Okay. Lyla is absolutely not wearing checkered pants and a white coat.

I look back down the bar at the girls. "Sasha?" I ask.

"Sasha. Mmm, even her name is delicious." He looks down the bar wistfully before slapping a hand to my back. "Wait. You know her? Dude, can you… Help me out here. I *need* to meet her. Introduce me."

I shake my head, my focus singularly aimed.

Lyla looks up, then darts her gaze away, like I caught her doing something she's not supposed to, but she's doing a shit job at suppressing her smile. If she's not careful, she's going to bite right through that lip.

As it is, she's abusing it pretty soundly, and all I want to do is pull the flesh from between her teeth and soothe it with my tongue.

"Is she coming this way? Raleigh, man, you *gotta* introduce me," John pleads. "Seriously, do this, and I'll cover for you next time you fly home to see your wife and kid, give you an extra day or whatever."

That offer is too tempting to pass up, but I don't bother to correct him on Laney. So, when Lyla and her roommate slide up behind us, I introduce Sasha to John.

And as much as I'm looking forward to an extra day with Matty, Lyla's the one who's got my full attention at the moment.

"Hey."

I had no idea someone could put so much bubbly enthusiasm into a single syllable.

She's doing that thing where she practically bounces with happiness. That bouncing that launches her boobs into motion and puts thoughts of all the dirty things I want to do to her front and center.

"Hey. I didn't know you'd be here." *No shit.* Now I sound like a moron because, of course, I didn't know she was going to be here. Why the hell would she feel the need to tell me her plans? We're neighbors. That's it. "Not that you need to clear that kind of thing with me."

For the love of fucks, could I just shut up right now? I'm starting to babble like her.

"Yeah. Sasha and I were going to grab a bite, but she got called in to cover for someone tonight, so I thought I'd come hang out with her brother's friends." She looks back toward the guys down the bar and then turns her pretty pink smile on me, full blast.

"Her brother's friends are in The UnBroken?" I ask.

"Actually, her brother is Gavin Keller. You know their music?"

"The guitarist is Sasha's brother? Holy shit. Yeah, I know them. I mean, I don't *know* them, not like you do, but I saw them live over the summer." I sound like a fucking teenager with a crush on the rock stars.

Ian Scott, the drummer, beckons Lyla back down there, biting at the hoop through his lip.

She holds up her pointer finger to him and turns back to me. "I guess Ian wants me," she says, and instead of that good feeling in my chest from moments ago, I swear to God, it feels like acid, burning and sour.

"Oh. Yeah, so you and Ian…?" I leave the question hanging because why the hell do I care? It has nothing to do with me. Not my business.

Lyla puts her hand on my arm and starts to laugh.

"Ian? Oh my God, no. He's great— super sweet— but no."

Her hand is warm on my arm, and I flex a little. The tightening of her grip, the widening of her eyes, are exactly the reaction I'm looking for.

I shift in my barstool, so I can face her head-on. And of course, that shift makes me flex a little more. Strictly a result of the movement, and nothing at all to do with peacocking it up for her or anything.

"Why's that? He an asshole? A player?"

"N-no. He's, uh… not that I know of. I just, um, not him."

I freaking love that I have the queen of non-stop commentary, stuttering to answer a simple question. And I hate it that when she pulls away the spot on my arm where her touch had been burning me, is now cold and empty.

"Excuse me." She smiles, making her way back down to talk with the guys. And I swear, my heart drops when the two famous rock stars wrap her up in a protective bubble. And then Kane fucking Newton, the lead singer, throws me shade.

Eight

Lyla

Surrounded by rock gods and no way to break free.

Some girls would think of that as a dream come true, but Ian and Kane are driving me crazy. I have two brothers of my own. I sure as hell don't need these two fools acting the part.

No, thank you. That's not the life for me.

I push free of Ian's colorful arm draped across my shoulders, only to be pulled tight to Kane's side.

"Would you stop it?" I wiggle and squirm, managing nothing except losing my balance. Pitching forward, I land even more solidly against Kane, close enough that his chuckle ruffles my lock of hair that forever seems to break free of its binds.

Kane reaches up, tucking it neatly behind my ear, and a sound that is distinctly growlish rises above the din of conversation from halfway down the bar.

A flash of green and black flannel passes by heading into the back hallway of the restaurant.

"Who's the man-candy, LD?" Kane drawls, singularly focused on Raleigh's ass. Sam is right, that ass does an amazing service to a well-fit pair of khakis. "You think you might want to introduce me to him? Is he a fan?" Kane licks his lips, and Ian just chuckles away.

Righting myself, I try to pull up some kind of dignity and shove Kane in the chest. "Nope. Shake that thought right out of your pretty little head," I tell him.

"Why?" he asks, rubbing a thumb across his lower lip.

On Kane, the move is one hundred percent sexual. And even though it seems *everyone* is Kane's type, he's absolutely not mine.

"Just don't, okay?" I don't like Kane lusting after Raleigh any more than I like Sam's commentary on him.

Ian takes a pull from his draft and shoves Kane's shoulder. "Our girl has a crush, man. Back off."

"What? I do not." I don't.

"And it's reciprocated. Did you see the way he was looking at her? Hear that guttural growl? Dude is staking his claim," Ian says, nodding back toward the restrooms where Raleigh disappeared. "You don't stand a chance, Kane. He's straight as an arrow and only has eyes for our girl, here."

Kane shrugs as only Kane can do. "I can work with straight. I've mussed up a lot of 'straight' guys who were just fine with a dalliance. It's not like I'm looking to out him. I just want to lick him. Bite a little. Make him moan."

"It's a magnificent sound," I say wistfully.

I'm only a little bit ashamed to admit that after Sam told me he was at the shop every morning, I started stalking. And, Lord have mercy, the sound he made when I brought him dinner before the hockey game. That was enough to set my face on fire. And other body parts.

"Oh, Miss Dupree. Do tell," Kane prompts.

Ian, on the other hand, gives me a hard look, a big brotherly one.

I roll my eyes at both of them and put a little more space between us.

"He comes into my coffee shop every morning. And I brought him dinner once, evidently a very good dinner. One he thoroughly enjoyed."

"What's holding you back, Lyla? He obviously has it bad for you," Ian asks. He's been nothing but sweet when we've hung out. Attentive and concerned, but truly, never in a romantic kind of way.

"He most certainly does not have it bad for me. I piss him off more often than not because of my stupid smoke alarm, and I can't seem to ply him with sweets." I put my hands up in front of me as they both try to jump on an innuendo there. "Thanks, but no thanks. I don't want to hear it."

And Kane just can't manage to hold himself in check. "Maybe you haven't been offering the right kind of sweets, have you thought of that? Maybe your presentation of said sweets is lacking." His gaze blatantly drops to my chest, and he waggles his eyebrows ridiculously.

Where Ian is attentive and sweet, Kane is so often dismissive; looking past what or whoever is right in front of him in search of the next plaything. He's a manwhore in every sense of the term.

"I think you're reading it wrong, LD. That man has it bad for you." Ian leans back and smiles broadly, the silver ring through his lower lip glinting as it catches the light above the bar.

His fans go out of their minds for that little hoop, and the way he pulls it into his mouth with his teeth. But that's a whole other story.

"Whatever. I'm out of here, guys. I'm going to go say bye to Sasha and bolt." I grab my coat and turn on my heel. "Just make good choices and leave Raleigh alone, Kane. He's off-limits."

"So, you're calling dibs?"

Instead of responding, I toss a wave over my shoulder and squeeze through an impossibly small gap in the now crowded bar and head down the hall at the back of the building. As I turn toward the kitchen to tell Sasha I'm heading home for the night, one of the restroom doors flies open, crashing into me.

I see stars and am sure that I'll never be able to move my shoulder again. That *might* be a bit dramatic, but it hurts. Bad.

When the stars all fade, I look up—following the black and yellow lines that weave through the softest deep green flannel—into gorgeous whiskey-colored eyes.

"I can't seem to escape you, no matter what I do," Raleigh grumbles, dragging his big hand down his face.

"Sorry. I shouldn't have been walking down this very public hallway," I bite out between gritted teeth.

I'm an utter contradiction right now. My shoulder is throbbing, my heart is galloping in my chest, and I might be a bit lightheaded from my proximity to his hotness.

Raleigh cringes a little and takes half a step back, putting space between us.

I close my eyes and take a deep breath, willing the bitchiness to leave me. "That was rude. I'm sorry. I'm just—"

Raleigh places his hand on my upper arm, and I wince at the pressure. "Shit, I'm sorry." He lifts his hand until it feathers over me, barely making contact at all.

"Are you okay? How badly did I hurt you?" he asks, stepping close to me once again.

"I'm fine. It's all good."

Raleigh steps even closer, pressing against me to let one of the restaurant staff get past us to the basement stairs.

The bartender pauses at the door and mouths a silent question to me asking if I'm okay.

I smile and nod, drawing Raleigh's attention away for just a moment.

He turns back to face me, the space between us nearly gone. "I didn't like seeing you wrapped up in another man."

He reaches up and slides my wayward lock of hair through his fingers once. Twice and then again, twirling it around his pointer on the last go before tucking it safely behind my ear.

"What are you talking about? I haven't been wrapped up in anyone for a very long time," I say.

My fingers seem to have a mind of their own as they slide gently against the softest flannel I have ever felt. I tuck a finger between the buttons, feeling the softness from both sides.

Raleigh's chest expands with a bracing breath, my fingers slipping even further inside his shirt. When he answers, his voice is lower than I've heard it before.

Strained and gravely. "Both of them—Ian and the singer —both of them had their arms around you. And then you smiled your big smile at them. The one that fills your face and crinkles your eyes. The one that pinks your cheeks."

His gaze wanders lazily across my face, pausing on each feature as he mentions it, before dropping to my mouth.

It's cliché as hell, but with the way he's staring at my lips, I can't help but lick them. And when I do, he pauses, holding his breath, watching intently.

"I... I..." The word stutters, caught in an endless loop in my brain. Or maybe I just can't think with him this close to me.

"And then the pretty boy—Kane—when he crushed you to his chest, the look he gave me. All possessive and shit. Practically pissing a circle around you."

I curl my hand around the buttons of his shirt, holding on tight. "He asked me to introduce the two of you," I whisper. "I think he's..." How do I even finish that?

"He's what?" Raleigh presses closer still, and my silly heart skips and dances.

"Interested," I say, barely breathing, focused on the tiny white scar on the edge of his lip. One that I hadn't noticed before from so far away. "In you. He's interested in you."

Time hangs between us, crackling and unmoving, dragging on into eternity.

"I'm not the least bit interested in what he has to offer," Raleigh says, his lips brushing against mine with each syllable.

And then the air shimmering around us combusts.

His lips against mine.

His fingers twisting and twining in my hair, our bodies crushed together. Nothing separates us from lips to hips, chest to the rest.

Our tongues tangle, teeth clash.

Our hands wander and explore.

We come together in the most delicious and decadent frenzy.

This kiss is all pent-up frustration and desire.

The world around us melts away, and instead of a dimly lit back hallway of a fantastic restaurant in trendy Manhattan, it's just the two of us exploring each other.

Learning each other.

Drinking each other in.

Until the sound of a throat loudly clearing pulls us from our heated cocoon of bliss. "'Scuse me," the bartender says, pushing through us, back toward the front of the restaurant. He mumbles something that sounds decidedly like, "take that shit home," but his thoughts and opinions are the least of my concern. All I see, all I want is Raleigh Jacobs, the grumbly grouchy mountain man, who's a little lost in the big city.

This should be one of those storybook moments, where the girl and the ogre have kissed and then fall madly in love. But sadly, reality is nothing like the fairy-tales, and now Raleigh won't look at me. His eyes are glued to the ground, only rising as far as my the tops of my boots.

As my heart pounds in my chest and my blood rushes hot through my veins, all I see is a waging war painted all over his features. I'm getting a severe case of whiplash from his swinging moods.

Discomfort rolls off of him in waves, swirling in the air between us. Frankly, this hallway isn't big enough for Raleigh, me, and whatever existential crisis he's dealing with at the moment. Something's got to give and without a doubt, the easiest thing to ditch is me.

He's struggling with something and struggling hard. His fingers rake through his hair, pulling at the longer strands on top. I liked it better when they were tangled in mine, but that's not where we are anymore.

A muscle in his jaw jumps as he grinds his teeth to dust. His nose wrinkles and his brows drop low over seemingly miserable eyes. Everything about him screams of the battle he's fighting inside himself.

My chest expands with a breath, and—making up my

mind to end this torture—I blow it out forcefully, telling him I'm going to go.

It takes a million years for his searing gaze to make its way from the floor to my face, stumbling over where my fingers rest against my mouth, holding the memory of his lips close.

Everything about him screams regret, and that, I just can't do.

When he finally meets my eyes, and I know I have his attention, I reiterate, "I'm going to go." And I turn my back on whatever that flip in him was and walk away, leaving him to figure his shit out.

Nine

Raleigh

I spent far too long in that restroom beating myself up for wanting what I shouldn't.

Lyla Dupree.

Her curves. Her attention. Her singular focus.

That's what I want.

That and to take the bartender's advice and take her home and lose myself in her. What the hell am I thinking? I can't do this.

I can't.

I push farther away from Lyla, resting my back against the wall opposite her. We're taking up way too much space in the tight hallway of a bar in Hell's

Kitchen. There are people an arm's length away, and here we were with our lips locked, hips sliding. I was practically dry humping her in public.

This is wrong. I push my hand through my hair and stare at Lyla's gray winter boots. Her boots are safe territory. If I look anywhere else, I'll be drawn back in and maybe, just maybe, throw her over my shoulder like a goddamn Neanderthal.

Don't be a Neanderthal, Raleigh.

I rack my brain, trying to think of the right thing to say. *I'm sorry* is totally wrong because I'm absolutely not. How can I be sorry for kissing her, for finally tasting her? It would be a complete lie and a dick thing to say.

I can't tell her that it was a mistake because God knows *that's* an even bigger dick-head statement, even if it might be true. I still have a couple months of sharing a wall with her, and I don't want things to be weird. And I don't want her to think I'm using her or just looking for a convenient lay. That's not me.

I thought I had the real thing with Laney, though it turned out I was absolutely wrong. I want to find something real and true.

Family. Special. Committed.

Commitment can't work long term in two different cities. And I have my son to consider.

"Wow. Maybe this, um… I should probably go," Lyla says, pulling me from my thoughts.

I rip my gaze from her feet, up her legs to her danger-ously curvy hips.

I will myself not to pause too long on the soft skin of her chest, the dip of her collar bone, her kiss-swollen lips and try to focus on her eyes. But I fail. Those lips—now that I've tasted them, I want more.

Her fingers flutter over them nervously, and when I reach out to still her hand, Lyla turns away.

"Yeah. I'm going to go." And with that, she walks down the hallway and through the door.

Fuck me.

I can't stand here, stuck inside my head, and just watch her walk away from me. I take off down the hall and through the door after her. If I get locked outside, I'll deal with it. I have to make this right.

Instead of finding the cold, quiet alley when I bust through the door, I find myself in the brightly lit madness of a perfectly orchestrated kitchen. And it doesn't seem to bother a single person that I'm here.

With a quick scan across the crowded space, I find Lyla. She's looking straight at me over Sasha's shoulder. I take a handful of steps in her direction, but she raises her hand, telling me to stay. And like the dog I feel I am, I obey.

The sounds of the kitchen—chopping and scraping, stirring and sizzling—make me realize how much I've missed cooking. I think the only real food I've had since coming to New York was when Lyla brought me dinner before the hockey game.

A waiter fills his tray with two piled-high burgers, fries overflowing the plates, and I wonder if those are going to the bar for John and me. I shift my weight and jam my hands deep into my pockets, so I don't check my watch. I've already made an ass of myself, no need to be an impatient ass.

"The kitchen is for staff only," Lyla says as she approaches.

"Yeah, sorry. I need to apologize, and then I'll go."

Her nostrils flare, her jaw sliding back and forth as she crosses her arms over chest. This isn't a look I've seen on Lyla. Bubbly and open has been replaced by stoic and closed off, not that I can blame her.

"I'm sorry for being a dick. For mauling you in public and then clamming up. I got a little lost in my head." I roll my shoulders and dip down to make sure she's looking at me, hearing me. "I'm not sorry for kissing you. But I don't know if that should happen again. I've got a lot of chaos in my life right now, and—"

"Totally get that," she says, not giving me much to go on.

"Okay. Excellent. Then I'm just going to—" I throw my thumb up over my shoulder and take a step back.

"Good plan. Enjoy your night." Lyla's brows rise high, and while she bites her lower lip like she always does, this time feels different, like she's biting it in determination of something. But what that might be, I don't know?

I'm a guy.

And I've already failed big in the relationship thing.

So, I nod and step back through the door and out to the bar.

I slide into my seat, and John gives me a chin lift as he devours his meal. I dig in and thankfully avoid conversation of the verbal kind. Anything I need to say for the time being can be conveyed with a nod of my head and the lifting of my empty pint glass.

John was right; the food is amazing. I wipe my mouth and toss my napkin on top of my empty dish, pushing it away.

Sated. At peace. Not a care in the world.

Two truths and a lie looks a lot more like two lies and a truth. There's nothing peaceful or carefree about me.

I push back and reach for my wallet. "Thanks, man. Food was great," I tell John, pulling some bills out and tucking them under the shot glass holding my tab.

"You're not leaving already?" John asks, beer foam clinging to his overgrown mustache.

If I were a woman, specifically a professional chef, there's no way I'd give time to a guy who wears his meals like that.

"What about dessert?" He turns in his chair and looks

longingly toward the kitchen. Dude has got it bad, and I just don't see it going anywhere for him.

"Yeah. I've got things I need to do, shit to take care of." I put on my coat and pull my beanie low on my head. "Thanks for dragging me out. I'll see you at work."

I don't wait for a response. And when I take one last look back toward the kitchen for Lyla, I'm met with the icy glare of a tatted-up drummer and a look I don't want to classify as interest from the singer of one of my favorite bands.

I'm not afraid of much, but that look from Ian Scott just about has me shitting my pants, so I get my ass out of the bar and head back to my building and the safe haven of my apartment.

I might be getting more accustomed to the rhythm and pace of the city, but I still relish the solitude of my place.

The relative silence. Relative being the operative term because as the elevator doors open, I hear the last pitiful bleat of Lyla's smoke alarm. One of the maintenance guys steps out of her apartment, a gigantic chocolate chip cookie in his hand.

Thank Christ, I missed the main event, though I'm sure that I could probably manage to sleep through the sound at this point. I pause in the space between our doors, my key digging into the palm of my hand, the warm scent of sugar and butter hanging heavy in the air.

Temptation.

I have no doubt—none at all—that I could have Lyla. Sink into her. Lose myself in her, but I don't want cheap and easy. I've had that, married it, and got the world's greatest kid out of it.

I wouldn't trade Matty for the world, but I don't want to do the superficial relationship again.

Next time I fall, I want forever.

Ten

That kiss.

My lips tingle for days and, despite how things ended the other night, I be-bop around like a love-sick fool. And maybe I am because regardless of the push and pull we have going, things are changing.

Sure, Raleigh comes off as rough and gruff and super cranky a lot of the time, but maybe we can just go with "rugged and reserved" now.

Somehow, that seems to fit him better.

The week skates by, each morning starting out a little more hectic than the one before as I get closer to making a huge life and location decision.

Sam thinks it's a good idea to let me know each time Raleigh walks in the door.

I can't disagree, though her methods, as usual, leave a little something to be desired. Shouting out, "dick in the door" is a bit much, even for the girl with no filter. "Sausage walking" isn't much better, and it takes some convincing to get her to simply bump open the swinging door and call for help.

But she does, and oh, is it ever worth the heartburn Sam causes me to see his face each morning, dark scruffy cheeks tinged pink from the early morning chill.

"Good morning, Raleigh. What can I get for you today?" I feel my own cheeks flush when he drags his gaze up the front of my apron, finally settling on my eyes after a brief pause at my lips.

"This isn't how we do this," he comments, nodding stiffly at Sam.

I tug my lower lip between my teeth to keep from laughing. He looks absolutely petrified.

"I promise, she won't bite," I answer, my cheeks pushing up into a smile that practically swallows my eyes. "Are you feeling something sweet this morning, or...?" I let my words trail off. Flirting isn't something I'm all that good at, and certainly not here, among the throngs of early morning patrons. That's just too big an audience for me.

"I, uh… yeah. One of those and—"

A steaming cup of his morning poison lands on the counter between us with a thump.

"You're welcome," Sam mumbles, already moving on to the next order.

"She's something else." He arches one perfect dark brow, his mouth pulling up on one side.

"She is." I carefully grab and package the muffin he indicated, watching as he wraps his lips around the black plastic top of his cup.

His tongue darts out, licking a stray drop.

When I blink myself away from pondering dirty thoughts, Raleigh's eyes are crinkled just a bit at the outside edges, like he's trying hard not to laugh, but he caught me.

Thank God, he can't read my mind. Who knows how he'd feel about being the star in my mental porn reel.

"See you later?" I ask.

He lifts his coffee cup as he walks out the door.

I'm not quite sure if that's a "Yes, absolutely, Lyla. I wouldn't miss it for the world" or "Meh. Maybe." I do know which one I'm hoping it means.

The bell above the door jingles, announcing his departure, and though there's a line all the way to that door and beyond, Sam is standing with her hands on her hips, staring at me.

In fact, she's staring so intently that, like a wave rolling through, everyone in the shop lifts their gaze and all focus is squarely on me.

Despite the early spring chill, a bead of sweat rolls down my back as I take in the scene before me. Honestly, the man's ass is a work of art.

I'm so not a fan of being the center of attention, which is why I love, love, love spending my time in the kitchen, creating.

Fine, I'm hiding back there. But who can blame me? So, I do what I do best and escape back to where I'm most comfortable.

Unfortunately, I curtsy as I back away into my safe space.

There's no way I can live that one down. And sure enough, the minute Sam swings through the kitchen door a while later, the first thing out of her mouth is, "What was that?"

I can't handle her judgmental judginess, so I drop my forehead to the Specials chalkboard resting on the counter in front of me. "I curtsied," I mumble.

The cooler door opens and closes. Bowls and utensils clang on the prep surface. And then there's a brief respite of silence before she says, "If you're going to do something dorky and stupid, at least own it."

I lift my head and sit up straight, staring Sam right in

the eye. "I curtsied. I fucking curtsied as I backed myself out of the arena of embarrassment. Is that better? Are you happy now?"

Sam looks up from the blade her hands are flying over as she slices brussel sprouts for the salad special today. "I'm a damn ray of happy sunshine every day, who are you kidding?"

I round the prep table and pull the food processor from its resting spot and plug it in. I feed the baby cabbages through the machine in a fraction of the time it took Sam to slice a scant handful.

"This is more efficient," I say as she scowls at me, proving herself full of shit on the happiness issue. "I got flustered, okay? I don't know what else to say. This is one of the many reasons you're here. I'm an absolute idiot when I'm out in the spotlight, among the people."

"But you're fucking brilliant in the kitchen. And I wouldn't have any reason to be here if it wasn't for you, so shut up and do your thing," Sam says solemnly. A rare event, for sure.

I shrug and pull another bin of washed veggies from the fridge, set it next to her and nod at the mandolin in her hand. "Work smarter, not harder. I'll go check on the customers out front. All two of them." I push through the swinging doors cringing at the wide-eyed look I get from the young guy in the hipster glasses at the table by the window. Was he here this whole time? Did he witness the awkward curtsy?

"Might want to wipe the pink chalk off your forehead," Sam calls after me.

I'm in serious danger of losing track of my embarrassment tally. I don't think this day can get any worse.

Somewhere on the subway, as the train sits unmoving for far too long, I curse myself for those famous last words.

I should have thrown salt over my shoulder. Knocked on wood. Sacrificed a chicken—well, a chicken salad sandwich because if truth be told, I prefer to think of meat coming from the grocery store or food supplier.

It's hard to swallow when you think about the fact that your meal used to have eyes and a soul. Maybe a family.

I drop a message into the family group chat to let everyone know that I miss them. I don't expect a response because of the time difference, but that doesn't mean I'm not hoping for one. A little distraction from my current situation would be more than welcome.

At least I thought it would be welcome. But between the responses popping up, my mother makes sure to get in a dig, commenting that maybe I could follow a boy home sometime soon.

And when my youngest brother sends a picture titled *Wish you were here,* my mood takes another dive. It's the view from a chair lift, framing tall pines heavily laden with fresh snow and just the end of his snowboard.

I peer over the top of my phone at the crowded subway car, the scent of various foods mixing with that of bodies crammed into too small of a space, creating what is uniquely New York. Looking back at his picture, I try my hardest to remember what clean air smells like.

Raleigh. It smells like my neighbor. Somehow, someway, the fresh clean scent of Colorado clings to him no matter how long he's been in the city.

I close my eyes, counting backward from one hundred and cataloging all the rugged perfection that lives on the other side of my wall.

Temporary or not, I could get lost in him.

Of course. Of-freaking-*course.* The day I decide to come home and bake instead of staying at work, I swear the alarm goes off with nothing more than a sideways glance from me.

Fine. The oven is on, but I *swear* I didn't spill even a crumb on the floor of the stupid appliance.

It makes no sense, none whatsoever, and though I know it's foolish, the thought tumbles through my head yet again. *This day can't get any worse.*

If I eat out—or get takeout—one more time, I might lose my ever-loving mind. I just can't. Sure, the pizza in New York is better than anything I've ever had, but I can't keep living on that and dirty water dogs indefinitely. I need a meal, actual home-cooked food with meat and vegetables and, hopefully, some leftovers.

I breathe a sigh of relief as the revolving door of my building encapsulates me, deadening the street noise, and shuttling me into the quiet lobby.

"Thomas, how are you?" I nod to the doorman on my way to the elevator.

"Well, sir. I have a delivery for you here. Shall I bring it up to your apartment?"

He ducks into the room to the left of his desk and comes back with a box. The sight of dancing vegetables on the side actually pulls at the corner of my mouth, not quite, but almost a smile.

"Thanks, man. I'll take it," I say, reaching across the desk.

Dinner is served.

At least it will be as soon as I throw together one of the meal-kits I ordered. I can practically taste the carne asada tacos, or maybe I'll go with the chicken alfredo. I don't remember what the other meal I ordered is, but it doesn't even matter. I'm eating like a king tonight.

"Are you sure? It's no prob—"

Excited at the prospect of chowing down on the tacos —because it's absolutely going to be the tacos tonight—I snatch the box from Thomas's grip and start across the lobby.

"I've got it, man. Thanks," I call over my shoulder, hitting the up arrow on the wall. And when the elevator doors open up immediately, I really do smile. In fact, I grin from ear to ear, practically dancing with excitement. But I push that shit down and keep my chill, because dancing in the lobby would require me to hand over my man-card, and it's absolutely something that the happy baker would do.

So, I absolutely will not.

Until the doors slide shut and then, I let loose.

Full smile in place, I dance to the bastardization of whatever instrumental song is piped into the elevator car.

I fully regret that decision when the car stops at my floor, and the doors slide back, revealing Sasha hoisting a full laundry basket from inside her apartment, the door propped wide open with a full view of the man dancing with his *Hello Veggies* box.

Me. A full view of me dancing with my stupid meal box.

Thankfully, Sasha's essentially got her back to me, but Lyla's got the million-dollar view. Of course, she does.

I wipe the grin from my face and dig deep in search of my dignity. Nodding, I juggle the box as I pass their door, getting my key in the lock and escaping into the silence of my apartment, leaving the bark of laughter behind me.

I don't care. I'm not going to let the chronically happy chick with the mixing bowl in her hand mess with my good mood. Life would be so much easier if I didn't have to fight an erection every time I see her or hear the damn smoke alarm from her apartment when she bakes.

I should just let it go already. Temporary is not what I'm after. I want a permanent, lasting relationship, not a fling.

After shedding my coat, boots, and rucksack, I slice open the box. Each meal is neatly organized in its own self-contained unit with all the required ingredients and the directions.

Simple and quick, tacos are the perfect steppingstone into finally cooking for myself again. I tuck the other kits in the fridge and bust into the box for tonight's feast.

Hands washed, I pull a pan from the cabinet, a cutting board, a knife, and then stop dead in my tracks. Why the hell are there so many little packets in the box? I read through the directions as I dump the miscellaneous shit on the counter.

"The fuck?" I say, grumbling.

This is supposed to be simple food, made fresh. That's their slogan. And it's a damn lie. There is nothing simple about the fuck-teen different steps to making these tacos.

Meat. Spice. Cheese. Tortilla. That's all it should be, but no. I've somehow ordered the taco kit from hell.

My growling stomach checks my attitude, and with a resigned sigh, I start the prep work. Mincing, chopping, dicing, swearing.

Marinating? I'm not fucking marinating shit. I'm starving and I just want my dinner. Can you say *hangry*?

What difference is it going to make if I skip a couple steps and move this thing along? All the spices and flavors are in there, right?

I set the skillet on the stove and crank the heat. Smoking hot is what they call for, temperature-wise. And when the air above the pan is shimmering with heat, I drop the seasoned meat in and give it a stir. I grab a beer from the fridge, because what else would I have to drink with tacos?

As the bottle top releases a *sssshhtttt*, the fucking smoke alarm starts blaring.

God damnit. Can we not get through one day without her trying to burn the building down? Or announce the fact that she's baking again? For the love of fucks…

I take another swig of my beer, stirring the steak, and it hits me. The alarm blaring is mine, not Lyla's.

I drag a chair over to the wall and step up, hitting the button the second I can reach it. But the noise keeps going. I curse under my breath and try to pry the smoke alarm open to pull the battery, but it doesn't budge. Between the blaring alarm and the pounding on the door, I can't fucking think, so I smash the detector with my boot and rip it from the wall as it lets loose with its dying squeal.

I drop off the chair and run to the stove, sliding the pan from the hot burner, killing the heat at the same time.

More pounding rattles my door and, embarrassed, I realize this isn't strictly a karma moment. It's not necessarily just my next-door neighbor I'm annoying with this bullshit, but the entire floor. Surely the other residents will all assume that it's just Lyla again, right? I mean, why would they think anything different?

I pull open the door, and of *fucking* course, just about every person on the floor has their door open and is staring straight at me. I don't like to think of myself as a blusher, but my face flames at the attention.

I wave the remnants of my smoke alarm at the gawking faces and call, "Sorry," over the head of the usual offender.

She's right in front of me, hair piled high on her head, apron tied tight around her tiny waist, and a white conical bag twisted in her hand. A metallic glint winks from the end of the bag as Lyla shifts her weight. Her ever-present sugary sweet scent is layered with chocolate again.

Pissed that I notice the different aromas, I ask, "What's the matter? My alarm bother you?" Like the hangry asshole I am.

Before she can answer, the elevator doors slide open, and Josh steps off, automatically heading in our direction without even looking up from his phone.

Surprise hits his face as he realizes it's not Lyla's apartment, but mine. His eyes drop to the busted white plastic dangling from my hand and he turns back to the elevator, saying, "I'll see if I've got a replacement in the shop. What is it with you two?"

My gaze lands back on Lyla as she shifts her weight and huffs that damn piece of hair away from her face.

"You've made your point, okay. The alarm is obnoxious, but it's not like I do it on purpose," she rambles away. If I'm honest, her rambling has kind of grown on me, but today, I can't take it. "At least our neighbors know when my alarm goes off, they're going to get dessert." She waves the hand holding the bag down the hall, gesturing toward each and every head still poking out of their doors staring at me.

The scent of chocolate swirls through the air around her. How is she so damn sweet even when she's being a petulant little sass-hole?

The lone closed door in our hallway opens, lighting me up with another judgmental glare. Or maybe it lights a fire under my ass, but whatever. I can't take it anymore, so I pull Lyla into my apartment, hoping the slamming of the door drowns out her gasp of surprise.

As soon as the shock wears off, she starts in on her verbal vomit again.

"I don't know how else to say I'm sorry about the alarm. I've apologized, I've brought you sweets and treats and… and… and you keep telling me you don't eat sweets, but we both know that's a lie. Because what kind of person doesn't eat cookies? You're a monster, right now, you know that? A grumpy"—she pokes me square in the chest—"growly"—poke—"monster."

Another poke is followed by a gentle shove against my chest. I have a feeling she didn't mean for it to be gentle, because she doesn't seem like she's in the mood to take things easy on me. I'm sure she put all the anger her five feet four inches can muster into that shove, but let's face it, there's not a lot of power there.

Or maybe it's that there's not a lot of anger. She is literally the sweetest, bubbliest person I've ever met, but this girl has *got* to shut up.

As usual, her rambling has put me into some sort of a trance. She's still ragging on me, and I haven't even heard the litany of my shortcomings and failures she's currently running through.

Her cheeks are flushed pink, her eyes wide and expressive. Her chest heaves as she sucks in more air to lay me even lower. And, Jesus, her cherry-red lips. The only thing that stops them from ripping into me is a quick swipe of her tongue, darting out, wetting them.

Silence.

I need silence.

So, I do the first thing I can think of, and I kiss her.

Slam my lips onto hers. And there it is. Sweet, beautiful silence. The only thing I feel is her soft pillowy lips, and that hand that was shoving at me is now fisted in my shirt. My head is filled with the raging thump of my heart and the blessed fucking stillness. No alarm, no rambling dissertation, no shitstorm at work. Just nothing.

The kiss does what it's supposed to, but damn if it doesn't last long enough. And let me be perfectly clear, it absolutely doesn't.

Way too soon, Lyla pulls back from me, releasing my shirt as she does.

"What do you think you're doing?" She huffs the words as her hand flies through the air, palm open, heading straight for my chest again. I catch her wrist in mine and spin us, pinning her hand to the wall above her head.

"Shutting you up," I growl.

It's not nice, and I instantly feel bad. We've both obviously had a rough day, and I'm being an absolute dick.

Like clockwork, her other hand flies, but this time, when I grab it, and that fucking white bag, and pin it next to the other one, a glob of chocolate drips from the silver tip. I watch as it falls in slow motion, landing on the upper swell of her breast.

Lyla pulls at her hands, trying to wiggle free, but all she accomplishes is another well-placed chocolate drizzle. She stills and I lean in, licking my lower lip.

"What… you… don't…"

I lower my head and lick the frosting off her creamy

skin, pulling a gasp from her. I lick and suck until there's not a trace of chocolate marring her ample boob.

"You said you don't like sugar," she says, her eyes focused intently on mine.

"I think I changed my mind," I growl, dropping my eyes back to her tits.

We're so close that, with each inhale, our chests meet between us.

So close we're breathing each other in.

So close, I can still taste her.

A grin pulls at her cheeks, but she tries to squelch it by biting her lip.

I want that lip. I want to lean in again and suck it between my own, biting and nipping until it's swollen and red. I lean in and feel the muscles of her hand shift and tighten.

"Oops," she says, a fake pout slashed across her pretty mouth.

A sweet dollop of chocolate lands in the middle of the red patch on her skin where my stubble marked her the first time I licked her clean.

And with another squeeze, Lyla maps a trail in chocolate, guiding me to fucking paradise.

Game on.

Twelve

Lyla

A nger.

Arousal.

Flirting.

Fucking.

It's a natural progression, right?

I was pissed when I came over here. Rough day on the subway. Missing my family. Stress over huge life decisions. All of that put me in a foul mood. But when I saw Raleigh all flustered and blushing, and then the way he moved me and pinned me against the wall, licking me.

Licking. Me.

For the love of God, I'm shocked at myself for giving my piping bag a little squeeze. *Why does that sound perverted?*

And then one more.

A smirk hits his lips, and Raleigh dips down, trailing his tongue through the chocolate, laving, tasting, sucking at my skin. He kisses across my collar bone, paying extra attention to the little dip at the top.

A moan escapes me, and he chuckles against my neck, his warm breath and scruffy beard lighting my skin on fire.

He releases my hands and lifts me up in his arms in one fluid movement. My ass lands on the island in the kitchen, right on the edge, where I have to wrap my legs around his waist to keep my balance.

Raleigh takes the pastry bag from my hand, the twisted end loosening in the transfer. "How the fuck does this thing work?" He squeezes it—*still sounds dirty*—and while a big messy glob pools at the hem of my shirt, a little bit escapes through the twisted end and dribbles down his hand. He sets the bag on the counter next to me and reaches for the dishtowel.

I grab his wrist and bring his hand between us.

"It takes finesse," I say, darting my tongue out to taste the glaze. "Years of practice, a delicate touch"—I wrap my lips around his thumb sucking it clean—"but you don't seem to have what it takes."

I look up at him through my lashes. I may never have had much luck with flirting, seduction, but right here, right now, this seems to be working.

Raleigh mumbles, "Fuck delicate." His other hand gripping tightly on my hip, fingers pressing into the soft flesh there.

"Yes, please," I say. Does dirty talk really work? Do I sound like I'm trying too hard?

His gazes bounces back and forth, focusing on one eye and then the next, searching. "Is that what you want?" he asks.

I lean back, putting just enough space between us to pull my chocolate marked shirt off.

He slides his thumb along my cheek, where I smeared dark chocolate glaze in the process. He holds his thumb to my mouth, eyes blazing.

I guess I didn't do so bad with that attempt of flirting.

I oblige him and lick the chocolate clean, sliding my hand to his waistband, wrapping my fingers around the buckle of his belt.

My nails graze along the skin of his stomach, the muscles clenching and tightening as he sucks in a gasp of air and holds it. Waiting. Anticipating.

Time stretches between us. Probably only the beat of a heart, or maybe two, but it feels like an eternity. Like a vacuum. Like nothing and too much all at the same time.

I tug ever so slightly, urging him closer.

His fingers sink into my hip so hard, so desperately, there might be marks.

I can't say I'm mad at the idea of that, so I fist my hand in his shirt and tug at both points of contact.

The thought flashes through my mind—maybe he doesn't want this. Maybe he hasn't moved or responded because he's back to fighting that stupid inner battle he was dealing with in the dark hallway of Kitchenne. Jesus, if I could melt away and disappear at this moment, I'd do it.

I resist the impulse to babble my way out of this and loosen my hold on him.

That tiny release spurs Raleigh forward in a flurry of frantic hands. Sliding his thumb from my mouth, he wraps his hand around the back of my neck, tilting my head and crushing his mouth to mine.

Soft lips, nipping teeth.

Cradling my head, he pulls me to the edge of the counter, snug against him. Perfectly aligned, he leans over me, guiding me until my back makes contact with the ice-cold granite.

I arch, minimizing the contact, or maybe maximizing contact with him.

Raleigh reaches behind me, and with the flick of his fingers, my bra releases. He slides the lace from my arms and tosses it over his shoulder where it flutters to the floor. Raleigh groans, his eyes hungry as they roam over my curves. And like he's flipped a switch, or given himself tacit permission, he becomes a blur. A man possessed. He's on a mission, and that mission is me.

I don't even notice the cold granite on my ass as my leggings and undies join my other clothes on the floor. Turns out, his chest is a perfect distraction, all taut muscle, a light dusting of hair.

He licks and kisses and bites—he flipping *bites*—his way across my chest, down my stomach and, oh sweet mother of God, the way his hand grips my ass as his tongue swipes and circles my clit.

My fingers splay wide across the countertop as a life-changing shudder moves through me.

My eyes roll back in my head, my heart stops—it's entirely possible that I'm having an out of body experi-ence, except that I am most certainly feeling *everything* he's doing to my body. An embarrassing whine slides from my lips as his mouth leaves me.

"The only thing sweeter than your chocolate crois-sants is this sweet-as-fuck pussy," he mumbles, licking his lips.

Brows pinched together, I lift up on my elbows just as his jeans fall away, and he sheathes himself. I swear he's still rolling that condom on as he thrusts into me. My breath catches as his hard cock fills me.

But holy hell, Raleigh takes me places I didn't know were possible.

I see lights. I taste hot man, beer, and myself mixed with a hint of chocolate. The faint scent of tacos. And the fluid feel of my limbs—completely and utterly new territory.

Full and aware.

Shuddering and shaking.

And when I think there's no possible way it could get any better, because really, nobody *actually* orgasms just by penetration, no matter how good the D, my world comes undone.

I don't know if I blackout for a moment or truly experience the *petit morde*, but when my eyes flutter open, the expression on Raleigh's face is one of pain mixed with bliss, eyes squeezed tight, mouth slightly open. And that sound he makes, there is nothing sexier than that guttural groan.

I push myself up, reaching out to smooth my fingers through his beard, and he slides a hand up my back, supporting me. Thank God, because, let's face it, pastry chefs are not known for their ripped abs and amazing muscle tone.

Raleigh blinks rapidly. He sucks in a huge breath and then blows it out, bowing his head until his forehead rests against my chest, his arms wrapped securely around me. It's an intimate moment, far more so than anything that's just happened, including the fact that we're still fully intertwined.

"I'm sorry," he says, his lips brushing against my sweat-dampened skin.

Here I am, literally balancing on the edge, mind blown, catching my breath with the man's dick still in me, and he's apologizing.

I wriggle my hips, trying to back away, remove myself from *everything*, but he just holds me tighter.

"Don't."

It's all I can think to say. I never expected this to happen, let alone for it to turn into *something*, but an apology? Nope. Not going there.

He sighs and lifts his head, focusing completely on my eyes, not just looking at me, but looking into me.

"I'm sorry for being a dick. I've been an asshole, jerking you around for weeks, months, and then… *this.* I have to apologize. I owe you that at the very least. Hell, I didn't even—I don't know—buy you dinner before I fucked you on the kitchen counter." That pained expression is back on Raleigh's face, but this time it's lacking the bliss.

How awkward is this?

"Pretty fucking awkward, honestly," Raleigh says. "Hang on, though. Don't… Just stay there a minute."

He pulls up his jeans and goes to the sink and wets a cloth.

Evidently, I asked that out loud.

"Does it help at all that I made tacos? It's not much; it

sure as shit isn't how I should have done this, but do you want to stay and eat with me?" he asks, handing me the warm cloth while he takes care of the condom.

I clean up and pull my leggings on. As I hook my bra into place, a soft gray t-shirt slides over my shoulder, fingers trailing lightly down my spine.

His touch is gentle and sweet, tender, and the complete opposite of what I thought I saw coming from Raleigh.

My head is spinning.

"Thanks." I pull his clean shirt over my head, pausing to inhale as I do. I wish it smelled more like him, but all I get is detergent and maybe a hint of pine that seems to cling to everything he touches. "I don't want to impose. I stormed over here pissed off at the world. I'll just—"

"Please stay," he says. "Unless you don't like tacos."

The muscles of his back flex and bunch as he reaches into a cabinet above his head for plates. He turns and looks at me expectantly, waiting for an answer.

Let's be completely honest, there's only one right answer. It's tacos.

"Is that a thing? Are there really people who don't like tacos?" I ask painting on a smile. Then, turning my back, I pat my curves. "This ass was built on tacos and pastries."

Raleigh chuckles, shaking his head at me. "Solid building blocks. I like it."

He dishes up the food and pauses before setting the plate on the island. We both look at the spot where we just were. You know, *were.* "Maybe we should—"

I purse my lips and grab a cloth from the sink. "Yeah, let me just wipe this down."

Little by little, the tension swirling around us eases. We set up at the barstools, making our way through the pile of tacos and a handful of beers.

"Thank you. This was great," I mumble as I wipe my mouth.

"Absolutely. I really do wish I had done better with this though. I, uh"—he rubs his hand down his face, scratching his fingers through his beard—"I might be out of my element here."

"With me?" I ask.

He pauses, thinking for a moment before responding, "Just here."

Thirteen

Raleigh

I don't know what I'm doing.

It's been years since I've dated, and I'm sorely out of practice.

While I'd like to think that the dissolution of my marriage can be explained away in the neat little adulterous gift from my ex-wife, I know the reasons go much deeper.

Laney was turned on by luxury and haute couture, not hiking and breath-taking vistas. For the life of me, I can't figure out how she thought she'd find that with me.

This city is more her style than it is mine, regardless of the good parts I've found.

Well, the good part, singular. Because really, anything good that I've experienced here all ties back to Lyla.

Coffee.

Hockey.

Food.

She feeds my soul in more ways than just the most obvious. Who would have thought that the most annoying sound in the world would have brought the bubbliest human being into mine?

At least for now, because as much as I'm not looking for temporary, that's precisely what this is.

A few more months, and I'll be done here, heading back home just in time for some of the best parts of having the Rockies in my backyard. Breathing clean air. Exploring, hiking the mountains, camping on the weekends with Matty and… Lyla. And Lyla?

Does she hike? How does she feel about camping? Waking up surrounded by beauty and nature. Cooking over a single burner camp stove. Is that something she, with her culinary flair, can handle?

It hits me, just how much I don't know about her. I jot a list on the side of my graph paper holding an orderly line of calculations and sketches for the plans I've been checking for the past couple of hours.

Once again, the construction guys made a change on the fly, and now it's up to me to make sure the thing will work, as-is. It never ceases to amaze me that people think it's perfectly fine to veer off professionally sealed plans and not anticipate some blowback.

It's just my ass that's on the line if this project fails—nothing important.

My mind wanders back to Lyla. Where did she grow up? Is she a native New Yorker? She sure as hell doesn't come across as one. So many of the people who grew up around here just keep their heads down and power through the crowds to wherever it is that they're going. Lyla chats, and smiles, and meanders. Those don't feel like *born and raised in the city* traits.

Where did she go to school? Has she traveled? What does she wish for on shooting stars? Jesus, has she ever seen a shooting star? The light pollution here is outrageous.

I add things to my list of Lyla questions between checking drawings, busting through calculations, and running numbers. Thankfully, it looks like the changes can stay with minimal alterations.

Much as I would love to stick it to the asshole who opted to cut corners, I'd much rather get this thing done on time and close to budget.

My phone buzzes, skittering off a reference manual and onto the desk where the buzz sounds much more insistent. Laney's picture lights up the screen, so I reach deep for civility and answer as politely as I can. "Hello?"

"Raleigh, where are you?" Laney huffs, obviously annoyed.

"East Coast, still. What do you need?" So much for being polite.

She sighs loudly, and I can almost hear her rolling her eyes. "I know, but *where* are you? Your doorman isn't letting us go up to your apartment, and…"

"Wait, what? What do you mean? You're here? In New York?" I sit back in my chair and flip through the calendar on my laptop. Did I forget something?

"Yes, we're here—"

"We, who? What the fuck, Laney?" I start shoving my laptop and a handful of other things into my ruck. "What's going on?"

I can't begin to imagine what she's doing in Manhattan. Did I jinx myself by thinking how this is so much more her scene than mine?

And then, I hear it—Matty's excitement over being in my house.

"Matty, calm down. Give me a minute. Raleigh, I have a flight to catch. I need you to tell—What's your name? Thomas?—I need you to tell Thomas to let us into your place and to maybe keep an eye on Matty until you get back. Traffic is way worse here than I thought it would be, and if I don't leave now, I'm not going to make my flight," she seethes.

"What flight, Laney?" I throw my jacket on and sling

my bag over my shoulders. For the life of me, I can't figure out what the hell is going through her head.

"How long until you get here? I sent you a text this morning telling you we were coming. I explained it all," she whisper-shouts into the phone, obviously about to lose her shit.

"Looks like you're going to miss your flight then. It'll be close to an hour before I get there," I tell her, popping my earbuds in and transferring the call to Bluetooth. This is prime time for commuters, and it could easily take even longer. I check my text thread and hoof it to the closest subway station. Not a single unread message. "You sure you actually sent it? I don't have anything from you since last week."

Laney has a bad habit of fucking up on sending texts, either forgetting to hit SEND or sending shit to the wrong person. It made it hard to hide her affair from me when I started getting messages she meant to send to the guy she was fucking at work.

A smart person would pay a little more attention to who she was sending hook-up messages to. Not my ex-wife, though. Nope.

"*Shit*, Raleigh, I don't have an hour. What the hell are you going to do about your son?" Yeah, she didn't even bother addressing the fact that she screwed up again.

"I'm going to do my best to get home—to *my* son—as soon as I can. I'll meet you in the lobby, but for the love of God, Laney, why don't you actually hit SEND, so I know what's going on?" I'm about to disconnect when I see a message notification from Lyla. At least she knows how to work a messaging app.

> Lyla: There's the cutest little guy in the lobby talking to Thomas. He looks just like you.

"…swear to God, Raleigh. My car is here, and I'm leaving. I'll send you my return flight info, so you can meet me at the airport with Matty next weekend."

What the actual fuck?

"Hold up. Next weekend? What are you doing?" And now I'm one of *those* people, talking way too loud on the subway, so everyone has a front-row seat to my three-ring shitshow.

"I'll be back next Sunday. Just read your text," she bites out.

I'd gladly read the text if she'd fucking send the damn thing. Before she hits END, I hear her telling Matty to be good for the nice man, and that Daddy just forgot he was coming. And then, the call disconnects.

Fuck, fuck, fuckity-fuck.

I can't believe her. How can she think it's okay to leave our six-year-old son unattended in the city for an hour or more? This is not the same woman I fell in love with in college and married. Not the same woman who I held in my arms as she sobbed over a pregnancy test just a few short weeks later. When did things go sideways?

With no other choice, I text Lyla.

> Raleigh: Are you still in the lobby?
>
> Lyla: Nope. Just unlocked my door, why?
>
> Raleigh: I need a huge favor…

I call instead because this is just too much for messaging.

As soon as Lyla picks up, I launch right into begging. "Can you go back down to the lobby and give your phone to my mini-me? It's Matty, and his mom is jumping in a car as we speak to get back to the airport for a flight. She apparently thinks it's fine to leave him with Thomas until I get there."

Lyla is quiet for a beat.

I'm sure she's wondering what it says about me that I was married to such a horrible shrew.

"I didn't know he was coming for a visit."

"Me neither, but here we are. Listen, I'm on the train, but it's going to be at least a half-hour if not more until I get there. Can you take him up to your place and let him watch TV or something?" The elevator dings and I lean forward in anticipation of explaining all of this to my son. "Is he there? Is he—"

"Hold on," Lyla says, her voice fading as she moves the phone away from her mouth. It's faint, but I can still hear as she introduces herself to Matty and tells him that I'm on the phone.

After the shuffling sound of the phone changing hands, Matty's voice shakes a little. "Dad?"

"Hey buddy, how are you doing?" My shoulders tense, and I will the train to move faster.

"I'm okay. But where are you? Did you forget about me?" He sounds so small. So sad.

I could wring Laney's neck, but that'll have to wait for another day. Right now, my kid needs me.

"I'm getting there as fast as I can, buddy. But I need you to do me a big favor, okay?" He sniffles and gives me a small *uh-huh.* "My friend, Lyla, the lady who handed you the phone, needs some help. Remember when you called me, and the fire alarm was buzzing? Well, that was her. She thinks she's a cook, but I need you to keep an eye on her for a little bit until I get home. She… Do you think you can do that for me? I'll be there as soon as I can." I hold my breath, but like a trooper, Matty rallies and jumps to the task of helping like I'd hoped.

"I can do it, Dad. I'm good at helping." Excitement laces Matty's voice. The sound of him bouncing up and down bleeds through the speaker.

The next voice I hear pulls at a spot in my chest. A

spot I thought had died along with my marriage but seems to show itself when I'm around Lyla.

"You threw me under the bus, didn't you?" Lyla chuckles.

"I did. Totally did, but it was for a good cause," I say, and more of her laughter slides through the line. "Fifteen, maybe twenty minutes more, barring any subway stoppages. Do you need me to pick anything up for you from the bodega? Wine? Fresh batteries?"

"I've got this under control, but you should probably think twice before offering me alcohol and batteries," she says cheekily, an obvious smirk in her tone. And then the call ends.

A solid half hour later, the train doors barely open and I push my way through, shouldering past people in a way that I don't even recognize as me. I shove my hands in my pockets and walk with a sense of purpose, weaving along the sidewalk, setting a fast pace and jogging across intersections while the red hand lights up, and others stop and wait.

Horns blare, cabbies curse, and I have zero fucks to give.

I swing into the bodega just down from 48th Street and grab a bottle of wine to thank Lyla and some milk for Matty because there's not much beyond beer in my fridge. It's not until I push through to the lobby of my building, lights glinting off the revolving door's chrome, that it hits me. I've become one of *them*.

A New Yorker.

I shake off that grimy feeling on the way up to the seventeenth floor and knock at Lyla's door. It bursts open with the warm, delicious scent of chocolate chip cookies, a gorgeous smiling face, and the excited pounding feet of Matty running straight at me. Hands pumping, ready to jump into my arms. It's an absolutely idyllic scene in every way; one that nothing could possibly spoil.

Until there is.

The alarm bleats obnoxiously.

Lyla's eye's go wide with shock.

Matty stops dead in his tracks.

And then, he falls apart.

Helping out, making sure Matty was safe and sound and taken care of was the perfect way to show Raleigh that there's more to me than just a loud neighbor who makes a good cup of coffee and gives the occasional *bonus*.

And let's be honest, the good coffee has to be attributed to Sam. I freaking hope I can find another one of her in whichever city I expand *Bonne Chatte* to. And that decision needs to be made soon.

My financial advisor is pushing hard for Denver. The

numbers just make sense there. I would do it in a heartbeat if emotions didn't have to be involved.

My mother would be hard-pressed to acknowledge my moving back to Denver as the success it is. Instead, she'd get stuck in the loop that feeds her agenda—that I followed a boy east and when he moved on, I had to come home. All she cares about is the I-told-you-so factor.

Moms can be such a pain in the ass. Dads, on the other hand, are full of understanding.

"Come on, buddy, you've got to chill a little." Raleigh scoops up his son, soothing his tears even as my anxiety revs up because I ruined their big moment.

Raleigh sits Matty on the counter next to the sink and grabs a paper towel from the roll. With one hand keeping his son firmly in place, Raleigh dampens the paper towel with cool water and then swipes at the tears staining Matty's red cheeks.

My heart breaks when the sweet little boy I'd spent the better part of an hour with turns away from me and hides his face in his dad's chest.

"I'm so sorry, Matty. That silly alarm does that all the time," I apologize.

He peeks around Raleigh, hugging tightly to his arm.

I don't blame him, that arm is the stuff of my dreams. The way it feels. The solid muscle that makes it up.

Matty's not shutting me down, so I give him a little

smile. "I wonder if I have some milk." I tap my finger against my lips.

Raleigh looks over his shoulder at me, his brows pulled low, his gaze flitting to where my fingers rests. I open the fridge and pull out a jug of milk and grab a cup from the open shelving right next to it. As I pour some milk into the glass, Matty starts squirming, leaning far to watch me around his dad.

"And cookies?" he asks, eyes wide. He's practically laid out across the counter. "Do I get to have some of the cookies you made?"

Raleigh grasps Matty under his arms and swings him around, plopping him onto a barstool. "One. You can have one, and then we need to get some dinner in you."

Raleigh's voice takes on a definite dad quality. Soothing and a little softer than usual. He may not like it, but he understands that sometimes, you just need a warm chocolate chip cookie with fresh cold milk *before* dinner. That sometimes, it's the only thing that will make a bad situation better.

I slide a cookie onto a plate and place it and the milk right in front of Raleigh's mini-me.

"Want me to see what I have? I can cook us some dinner," I offer. When I get a "no" and "nope" from the men staring at me from the other side of the kitchen, I cringe. I throw my hands out to the side, asking, "What?"

Matty looks at his dad and shoves the rest of his cookie in his mouth, effectively throwing Raleigh under the bus to provide the explanation.

"I'll just order pizza. You've, uh, already done enough to help. We don't want to impose." Raleigh pulls his phone from his pocket and taps away, ordering dinner for them.

"Oh, okay." I scoop the rest of the cookies into a plastic tub and wash the baking tray.

Raleigh collects his son's things and guides him toward the door. "Thank you," he says, tapping Matty on the back twice.

"Thank you, ma'am." Matty wipes his hand across his mouth and hops on one foot around Raleigh. "See you later, gator."

He's so stinking cute. I love how kids move on so quickly from an unpleasant event.

I hand the bin of cookies to Raleigh and say, "You might need these."

I don't even think when I lean forward to kiss him. It just happens, but he takes a step back and glances at Matty.

"Thanks, really." The moment is awkward, both of us standing here, neither of us really knowing what to say.

I take a deep breath, ready to start in on what I normally do when I'm nervous, and then quickly pull my lower lip between my teeth to curb the rambling.

Raleigh's eyes drop to my mouth and stay there for a beat before continuing, "I need to get him settled, figure out how this week is going to work."

"Of course. Let me know if I can help." I put all of my bubbly personality out there, reverting back to when I was trying to win him over as a friend.

But what are we actually? Friends? More? At this point, I don't really have a clue, but I do know that I want it to be more.

When the door clicks shut behind them, my apartment feels quiet and way too empty. My go-to activity is out since there's no way I can bake away the blues. I'd scar that poor child for life if the alarm goes off again, and he's got enough going on in his world with his mom being flakey and dropping him here the way she did.

I pour myself some wine and burrow into the big chair by the window and look out over the city. It's so big out there—so many people in such a small amount of space.

How could a mom bring her child and leave him with a perfect stranger in a place he's never been? It's absolutely stupid and makes no sense at all. Wouldn't that be some sort of abandonment?

From what little Raleigh has said, she has primary custody—and with a stunt like she pulled today—I can't for the life of me understand why.

A short time later, a delivery guy knocks next door,

and the deep timbre of Raleigh's voice is muffled by the wall separating us.

I lean my head back and picture him taking care of his son. Setting him up in the second bedroom, getting him dinner, talking about flying to New York. Being a dad. I bet he's a really good one.

Not in the mood for my usual cheese and cracker dinner for one, I stand and take the rest of my wine to my room and get ready for bed. It's early still, but since I keep baker's hours, it's almost never too early for me to crawl between the sheets. I read for a bit, trying to lose myself in someone else's story, but it's just not working.

I plug in my phone and check the alarm before burrowing down in my blankets. Tomorrow is a new day.

My luck is nothing but bad. I have one alarm that won't shut up, and the other decided that today was a great day not to work. *I'm so late.* I jump out of the cab, making a mad dash to the *patisserie*. Thankfully Sam is already there, prepping things for the day.

"For the love of fucks, please tell me you have a good reason for running in here late. Looking like *that*." Sam hits the button on the coffee maker, brewing a huge carafe to start the day.

"My alarm didn't go off," I say, running my fingers through my hair, trying to tame the wildness into some sort of presentable order.

"Jesus. You and your alarms," she mutters.

There's no time to get into anything with her, so I push through to the kitchen and bust my ass getting my shit together, and that just sets the tone for the whole morning.

I feel like I'm constantly a step behind and not quite able to catch up. So when the call comes out that Sam needs help up front, I grumble and throw in the towel. Literally. Thankfully it lands in the sink and doesn't ruin any food or—God forbid—on the stove, setting off an alarm and putting me even further in the weeds.

I grab a fresh towel from the stack under the counter, wiping my hands as I push through the doors, expecting the line to be a mile long. It's well past my gorgeous neighbor's usual coffee time, but that's exactly who I see. Raleigh and Matty, dressed in jeans and jackets, matching beanies pulled low on their heads. Identical deep brown eyes and crooked smiles.

"Hey, boys. What are you doing with your day? Not working?" I ask.

Sam slides Raleigh his coffee and adds an extra dollop of whipped cream and a massive amount of chocolate shavings to a hot chocolate. I must be delirious because it almost looked like she smiled at Matty.

"Took the day off," Raleigh says tightly. "Thought we'd go to Central Park, see the zoo. Maybe grab a hotdog and a pretzel."

My heart squeezes at the thought of Matty getting to experience the city with his dad. Hopefully, Raleigh's hate of all things New York doesn't ruin it for him. I smile at the image in my mind of these two, walking hand in hand down the sidewalk, a pint-sized version of the original taking in all the new sights around him.

I pile several pastries into a box for them, tying the red and white string into a neat bow.

"Wanna come too?" Matty asks, bouncing on his toes.

"Careful, bud. Don't spill," Raleigh says, taking the cup from Matty's hands.

Now—free of all hindrances—Matty holds tight to the edge of the counter and jumps up and down, his little legs pumping. "Please. Please, please, please—"

Raleigh neatly stacks their cups on the pastry box and calms his son with a gentle touch and a look that stills the wildness of the moment. "Lyla has to work; she doesn't get to call in sick like me."

A sheepish grin crosses his face. This is a new look for him, one I've not seen yet—shy and patient.

While I'm lost in la-la land, staring at this man who just keeps getting better and better every time I look at him, I feel a tug at my waist. I swat at Sam's hands as she unties my apron and thrusts my jacket and purse at me. "Go. I've got this covered."

"What about lunch? That needs to be prepped, and you need help up here, and—"

She shoves me out of the way. "I've got this. You're going to have to let me do it on my own at some point, and we have the new chick coming in any minute," she explains as the bell above the door jingles. And in walks my new employee, Marta.

It took ages to find someone who Sam didn't scare off during interviews. But when Marta rolled with Sam's strong *personality*, I had no doubt about her being a good fit.

"Seriously, go on, LD. You need a day off. Honestly, make it two. If things get dicey, I'll call, or better yet, I'll deal with it." She pours another coffee and hands it off to me.

I've been booted from my own business. Kicked to the curb and told not to come back.

Raleigh holds my jacket out for me, sliding it up my arms. Never in my life has anyone done that for me. Never. And if I'm honest, I *really* like it.

With the box of pastries tucked under his arm, Raleigh guides us toward the exit. "Get the door for Lyla, Matty, and then you need to hold a hand."

"'Kay, but I'm holding Lyla's hand, not yours," Matty

announces, putting all of his weight behind pushing the door open.

Raleigh helps him out, a laugh only just escaping. "Whoa, why's that?"

With all the attitude a six-year-old can muster, Matty scoffs over his shoulder. "Duh, she's prettier than you." And with a big, old grin on his face, he slides his small hand into mine and bounces on his toes.

"I love it when he bounces like that," Raleigh says, stepping up to the curb to hail a taxi. One stops immediately, and we pile in, Matty nestled between us. Raleigh pops open the box of pastries and hands out the treats, licking his thumb and forefinger before grabbing a chocolate croissant for himself.

"It's adorable. Like barely contained excitement," I say.

When Raleigh doesn't respond right away, I glance at him and get caught in his gaze.

"I like it when you do it too. Just for different reasons," he says under his breath, a cocky smirk slashed across his face.

"That's it? Where's Alex, the lion, and the hippos and the giraffe? Where's Marty?"

The disappointment rolling off my kid is palpable. And yet, what did I expect? We're not going to find a real zoo here, nothing like the one in Denver or Colorado Springs. Or, hell, Omaha. That zoo is incredible.

"Sorry, buddy. We'll go to the real zoo next time I'm home. See the camels and the bears." I walk a little faster trying to think of some way to salvage the day.

Matty's a good kid, but this was a pretty big disappointment for a six-year-old. Hell, it was a disappointment to me.

In a matter of half a dozen steps, I'm alone on the path. What I see when I turn is Lyla and Matty standing together by the clock tower as the bronze animals dance and twirl to a nursery song. My son and the woman who blasted her way into my life are wearing matching expressions of delight.

She crouches down and takes his other hand, dancing with him in the middle of the park. Other kids join in, bouncing and laughing until the tune ends.

What could have been a meltdown is now a happy moment for my kiddo. And it hits me that this is the second time in as many days that Lyla has rescued us. Turned a bad situation into an adventure.

This is how life is supposed to be. Smiles and adventures. Baking cookies and drying tears. Walking hand in hand through the most disappointing zoo ever and making the best of it.

If I'm not careful, I could fall for her, and then what? She lives here; I don't.

"What's next? I think it's still too cold to drive the boats on the lake, but we could walk through the park and maybe try to find a playground, burn off some of the sugar?" Lyla suggests sweetly. So we do, and just like that, Lyla takes on the job of tour guide and entertainer.

We hit up a playground, grab a couple of hotdogs, and wind our way through the Museum of Natural History. And Matty's smiling and laughing the entire time. Through a museum. That shit has never happened. Normally, he'd be whining halfway through the exhibits. Of course, Laney would be bitching and whining too. But with Lyla, it's nothing but fun. Even as Matty winds down, reaching the end of his attention span for the day, Lyla rolls with it, damping the sparks of his discontent.

Admittedly, maybe the decision to walk home from the park after walking all day long was a mistake.

That was on me—all my fault. But we were so fucking close, it seemed a waste to grab a cab.

"I'm tired. I can't walk anymore." And the whining commences.

"We've hiked farther than this. You can do it," I say.

"But this isn't hiking," Matty whines, shuffling his feet. "I can't make it."

I don't want to be a dick or anything, but he most certainly can make it and will. For one thing, I can see the building from here. Also, if he stopped dragging the toes of his shoes with every step, he'd use a lot less energy.

I'm struggling to find the right words of encouragement when Lyla chimes in.

"You like to hike?" She pauses against a building to

tie her shoelace that was tied perfectly fine, giving Matty a break without making a big deal about the fact that she's giving him a break. "I love hiking. There's a place not too far away where you can go hiking through a zoo."

Lyla stands and reaches for Matty's hand, walking a touch slower, trying to distract him.

"That's not hiking. Hiking is in the mountains, and Daddy says there aren't mountains here. Right, Dad?"

"Yep, that's right. No hiking here in the city."

Lyla grins easily. "No, but just north of here. Less than an hour's drive," she explains.

And miraculously, Matty finds the energy to skip. He's skipping down the sidewalk instead of complaining of tired feet.

"How do you get there? Do you have a car? Where do you put it? How come you don't drive it to work?" Questions tumble out of him in a tidal wave, kind of like when Lyla rambles.

The way Lyla answers him—patiently addressing one question at a time—pulls at that spot in my chest.

Why did I find someone *now*? And why so fucking far from home?

"I don't have a car anymore, but I used to. It costs too much money to keep one here, and it's super hard to find a parking space. So, when I need to get out of the city and walk in the woods and visit the animals, I take a bus."

"I ride a bus to school, but that's different, right?" Matty screws up his face, maybe thinking about riding on the school bus for any reason other than going to school. Life in the city is so different from what he's used to.

Lyla agrees and then checks how close we are to home. She's been an amazing trooper today, but I can only imagine she's looking forward to some silence in her quiet apartment this evening. Maybe more of the cheese and crackers she seems to have for dinner more often than not.

"So, how do we get on the bus that takes us to the mountain zoo?" Matty's head is swiveling, busses passing in every direction. "How do you know which is the right one?"

Lyla explains the process and the bus station as our building comes into sight.

"Can we go? Right now?"

I have to laugh at the about face this kid has taken— exhausted and whining to ready to hop a bus and go hiking.

"Let's grab some dinner and table that discussion until later, okay?" I guide him toward the door to our building, and my heart swells with pride as he steps aside and tells Lyla that ladies go first.

In the elevator, Lyla leans back against the handrail. "Thanks for letting me tag along today. I had fun."

"Have dinner with us," I blurt out. So much for leaving her to unwind from today.

"That's okay. You don't have to—"

"Yes!" Matty pumps his fist and jumps out of the elevator the minute the doors open—on the wrong floor.

"Dude, get back in here. You can't just jump on and off the elevator," I chide.

"But Lyla's gonna have dinner with us, and then we'll go to that mountain zoo," he says as if one thing has anything to do with the other.

"Oh, Matty. I don't think your dad wants—"

I cut her off because even though I'm not sure what I want, I know I don't want this day to end yet. "Drop your stuff off and come over. I'll order Chinese, extra egg rolls?" I hold my breath until she nods her agreement.

We part ways at our doors, and I scurry Matty inside. "Wash your hands, soap and water, count to thirty while you scrub. And then come pick up your pjs—why are they on the coffee table anyway?"

Matty shrugs and hops on one foot to the bathroom. The neighbors downstairs will hate me by the end of the week. Maybe I'll ask Lyla for a box of pastries to apologize to them for the hopping noise.

With our food order placed, I straighten up the apartment—not that it's a mess—but I seriously don't understand why last night's pajamas are on the coffee table. And socks balled up and stuck on the television stand. I check the fridge, wishing I had thought to pick up some beer, when a knock sounds.

And just like that, Lyla's here, looking fresh and beautiful, a couple bottles of beers in each hand.

Over dinner—between Matty's wild ramblings and Lyla's slightly less wild ramblings—we somehow make plans for tomorrow. I rent a car because there is no way I'm riding on a bus through all the small towns Lyla describes to Matty, hopefully exaggerating just how tight the turns are through some of the villages.

"Don't want a story tonight," Matty mumbles through a yawn as he slides along the wall of the short hallway to his room. Poor kid is wiped out. I follow behind and get him all tucked in, his eyes shut before his head hits the pillow.

Bottles clink softly as they settle in the recycling bin, and when I step into the kitchen, it's absolutely spotless. Not a cardboard to-go container or a puddle of soy sauce anywhere. And no Lyla. She's gone.

I pop out into the hallway just as her door clicks shut. I stand here, leaning against the wall for far too long, staring.

Staring at nothing and thinking about all the things that just can't be.

I go back into my apartment and flop down in bed to

scroll through the pictures I took today. I stop on the one of Lyla and Matty dancing.

My son is laughing his fool head off, arms in the air, crouching low with his legs going in a totally different direction than the rest of his body. He's the embodiment of simple joy.

Lyla reflects his delight, magnifying it, and making it that much more special. She's just met him—barely knows him—but the way she goes out of her way to make his impromptu visit a memorable experience makes me wonder about what could be.

If only.

I thought there was no way yesterday could be topped, but after hiking through the Bear Mountain Zoo, filling my lungs with fresh mountain air, and marveling at the rosy glow on the faces sitting across from me, I know I was wrong.

This is perfection.

"What do you think? Was this a better zoo than yesterday?" Lyla asks over a bowl-sized cup of hot chocolate.

Matty nods, his cheeks puffed out around the huge marshmallow he shoved in his gob.

"What about you, Raleigh? Do you feel better up here in the mountains?" she asks me.

Nodding my head, keeping my eyes trained on her, I answer, "I do. Can't understand why people live in that concrete mess when all of this is right here. It almost makes New York doable."

Lyla huffs a laugh and sets her cup down. "What do you mean *doable*?"

"A house up here, trees and trails—I could handle this side of New York. If the schools are good, I would consider, I don't know, making a change." I rub at my beard and watch for her reaction.

Honestly, the best part of the state is sitting right across from me.

She glances over at Matty and smiles, sliding him the plate of marshmallows she ordered on the side. "That could be really hard."

I wait until her eyes are back on me before responding. "It could. But someone took pity on me recently and has shown me that there are little gems hidden in plain sight if I just look hard enough."

"You have a lot of factors to consider," she says, sliding her gaze back to my son.

She's right. I do have a lot to think about. A lot of moving parts and ripping Matty away from familiarity is not an easy thing. I don't know how to respond just yet, so I nod and finish my coffee.

I have to force myself to stay engaged for the rest of the day, to not get lost in possibilities and thoughts of how a move would work. I stay focused as we tour the Military Academy at West Point, just up the road. I stay involved as we grab something to eat at one of Lyla's friend's restaurants on the river. I stay one hundred percent with them as Lyla and Matty play goofy games in the car on the way back into the city. I'm still present as we return the car, ride the elevator up to our floor, Matty a dead weight in my arms and Lyla by my side.

It's not until I've got him tucked into bed with Lyla's help that I allow my mind to wander freely. I close his door behind me and pad softly down the hall behind Lyla.

"Thank you. Today was—"

"It was kind of amazing," she finishes for me.

"It was." I step into her space, crowding her against the kitchen island.

Her breath catches, and her hands land on my chest. That simple touch heats the blood pumping through my veins, filling me with desire while emptying me of rational thought. She curls her fingers, gripping my shirt in her fists as I run my lips along her cheek to plant a kiss below her ear.

"Stay," I demand more than ask when she shudders.

I'm not ready to let her go.

I trail kisses down her neck, tangling my fingers in the hair at the back of her head. The strands are like silk against my skin. I push her sweater off her shoulder and pull at the bright yellow strap of her bra. It's the color of sunshine and lemons.

Her nipple pebbles through the lace as I make circles around it with my thumb. Licking a lazy path across the swell of her breast, I pull it free and wrap my lips around her, sucking and tasting. Nipping and biting until Lyla moans.

I scoop her up intending to take her to my bed and explore every beautiful inch of her.

"Daddy. I don't feel—"

Whatever Matty was going to say ends up in a puddle of vomit all over the floor, the only thing that works faster than a cold shower.

Lyla rights her sweater and grabs a roll of paper towels. "Take care of him; I've got this," she says.

And by the time I've got Matty cleaned up and settled snuggly against my chest, our moment is gone.

"I'm going to go. Do you want me to run out and grab anything? Ginger ale?" She runs her hand across his forehead, pushing his hair back from his face, flushed with sleep.

"Nah. I think he'll be good now. Back to himself by

morning." I slide down on the couch getting a little more comfortable. "Thank you, Lyla. For everything."

She nods and lays a throw blanket over us. "Call me if he needs anything," she whispers and quietly leaves us alone.

It doesn't escape me that she put Matty and his needs first.

It seems that—like me—she would do anything for my son.

Sixteen

Lyla

"Ten minutes, Lyla. It took me just ten minutes to lose my son somewhere in the fucking building. And thank fuck, it was just in the building." Raleigh shoves his hand through his hair as he paces the length of his living room.

The "incident" happened the day before Matty's mom picked him up on her way back from her spring break vacay.

What grown-ass adult with a child goes away for spring break and doesn't take their kid?

I wanted so badly to go with Raleigh to meet her at the airport with Matty. I wanted to tear into her and give her something to think about on the rest of her flight home.

It's for the best that I didn't.

"Raleigh, he was fine. The Hendersons brought him right back up here to you. He just—"

Raleigh turns and glares at me.

I know the man is on edge. I know that he's really not fond of the city. And I am well aware of how much he loves his son and how much Matty means to him.

In all honesty, there is nothing in the world sexier or more attractive than a father's love for his child. But holy cows—and I do mean all of them—that glare of his is withering at best.

Without any conscious decision to do so, I take a couple of steps back, putting some much needed space between us and pull in a cleansing yoga breath. Four counts in, four counts out. I square my shoulders and do it again. Four in, four out.

"Raleigh." I put as much calm in my voice as possible, but it's pointless. He's wound up, and there's no soothing him with words.

Silently, he storms to his bedroom and starts pulling clothes from his drawers, from the closet, shoving them into his duffle.

"What are you doing?" I ask.

Piece by piece, I take his crumpled clothes from the bag and fold them neatly. It's so not my place, but I need something to do with my hands. I need a purpose, no matter how small and meaningless. "Matty's home, now. Safe and sound."

"And he's going to fucking stay there. What the fuck was Laney thinking, bringing him here and leaving him? It's too big. Too much bad shit happening here." He grabs a pile of neatly folded shirts and places them back in his duffle.

"What are you talking about? You guys had a blast while he was here. Up north, you said you could handle it, that it was a gem. You said… I mean, you implied…" My words off into nothing.

"Yeah, well, I was wrong," Raleigh barks out on a huff. "I was fucking wrong about all of it. Everything. There's not a goddamn thing worth a shit here. Nothing but people on top of people, fighting for space. Bad attitudes and filthy, disgusting sludge for air. I don't know how people fucking live here."

His words sting as they spew from his mouth.

I don't know why I do it, but I help him—actually help him—pull his clothes from the dresser and pack his things up to leave.

"Your project though. It's not done for another month or so, right? What are you going to—"

"It's far enough along, I can monitor it from Denver, finish things up from there. The person I care for the most in this world is there, so that's where I need to be. John can handle shit here. I'll fly in if I have to."

He zips his duffle closed and stalks to the closet where he pulls his stuff from the hangers and tosses shirts and pants, jackets and sweaters into his rolling suitcase.

This is really happening. He's leaving.

I stop—completely stop—what I'm doing, his gray Colorado hockey shirt clutched tightly in my hands. I lift his shirt to my face, burying it in the soft cotton.

I inhale the scent of clean laundry and the hint of fresh pine air that is distinctly Raleigh.

I have no right to be as upset as I am. I'm in no place to demand more of an explanation. I have no claim on him.

This was temporary. It was always just a temporary thing. And my decision to be his friend, to show him the good parts of the city were all self-imposed. He didn't ask for it.

Maybe he never really wanted it.

Maybe I just forced myself into his life, repeating history. Although I definitely had more with Raleigh than I ever did with the with the boy my mother warned me about.

Oh shit, my mother was right. Once again, I blindly grabbed hold of a man and inserted myself into his life, only for him to walk away when he was done with me.

I fall back against the dresser, Raleigh's t-shirt wadded up in my hand as he scurries around. Winding up his charging cords, tucking things in his computer bag.

Raleigh flips open his laptop and pulls up a travel site. "Fucking last minute shit. No flights until"—he scrolls and taps furiously, searching for any way out of here—"there we go. Flight 2129 leaves about eight tonight and gets in at ten local time. I can make that work," he mumbles.

His phone pings with a notification, and he's back in motion, clearing out his fridge— not that there's much in there—but it all goes in the trash. The trash goes out to the garbage chute. Everything in its place, like he was never even here.

Raleigh blows past me and pulls his bags through the apartment, setting everything by the door, ready to go.

Nothing left behind. Nothing at all.

I nod my head, not saying a word. Because what is there for me to say?

I blow out a bracing breath and walk with squared shoulders and my back ramrod straight to the door. I step around his bag, out into the hall, and through to my apartment.

The mail crinkles loudly as I plant my ass in the chair in the foyer.

Fifteen minutes. Twenty minutes—pass in a haze of

nothingness before I push myself into action. I wonder if he's even noticed that I left.

I fight the urge to be pissed and seek calm headspace the only way I know how. All my aggression goes into whisking and mixing. Beating the ever-loving fuck out of my egg whites before forcing myself to slow down and fold them into the mix with a gentle hand.

This is my happy place.

Baking.

Creating.

I set the timer and clean my kitchen, setting everything to rights. Calm from the chaos.

I open the oven, looking for the perfect golden-brown edges showing that it's done. And of course—of-fucking-course—the alarm goes off. I pop open my door to make life easier on whichever maintenance guy is on duty tonight and go back to dealing with my pastries.

The room goes quiet way too quickly for it to be anyone other than Raleigh.

"Jesus, I won't miss that at all," he says, sauntering into my kitchen.

"Evidently, you won't miss anything, Raleigh." I transfer my pastries to a cooling rack one by one, purposely avoiding him.

He crosses the small space and reaches out to pluck one from my spatula.

"Huh?"

How is it possible for him to sound like he's really perplexed? He can't be that clueless, can he?

"Just repeating what you said." I keep my voice even, giving him no emotion. And no pastries either. I take the confection from where he has it poised, ready to take a bite, and chuck it in the trash.

I don't want to look at him, don't want to show him how hurt I am.

I can't help but notice, out of the corner of my eye, how shock registers on his face.

Brows high.

Mouth agape.

I expect his cocky, grumpy attitude to fly, but Raleigh surprises me.

"What was that, Lyla?" He takes a step closer, and I take one back. "What's happening? Are we dancing, or…?"

All I wanted was to make a new friend, show a lost soul a little kindness, make a displaced person feel a little bit settled. I never intended to fall, never wanted to feel this… this… discarded again.

Hell, we've never even had a conversation about what this is, where it's going—or not going, for that matter.

"Lyla?" Raleigh dips down, so I can't avoid his eyes, so I can't avoid *him* any longer. "Talk to me, please?"

Sighing, I toss the spatula in the sink and plant my hands on either side of the empty baking sheet.

"All we've done is dance, Raleigh. Sometimes it's beautiful, sometimes angry. Flirty and funny, sweet and sexy. We've danced a million different dances to whatever tune happened to be swirling around us in any given moment. But the dance is done. The music has ended, and it's just time to curtsy or bow out." I smile sadly, remembering the morning I curtsied to him in the *Bonne Chatte*, and I take a step back repeating the motion. "Thank you for the dance, but it's obviously time for you to just go home," I say and walk out of the kitchen, head held high.

The front door opens, admitting Sasha, her arms laden with groceries and a couple bottles of wine. Her brows knit together as she glances from me to the man standing in our kitchen and back to me.

As soon as the realization hits her—because she's seen me through this kind of thing before—she gives me a small nod.

The first tears well in my eyes as I enter my bedroom. The first silent sob catches in my throat as I close the door to the sound of Sasha telling Raleigh he needs to go.

Their voices are muffled, but I can still hear bits of their angry conversation, and I really don't want to.

I pop my earbuds in, not even sure what music will help.

All I want is silence.

All I need is a big glass of wine and my best friend.

To mourn for a hot minute the fact that history is a bitch and that maybe, just maybe, I did it again. Fell when I shouldn't have.

At the very least, I'm thankful that I didn't gush to my mother about him, that the only ones who will know about this crash and burn are Sasha and Sam.

Lost in thought, and folding laundry with my silent earbuds firmly in place, I startle when Sasha opens my bedroom door.

"It's safe. You can come out now," she says, a bottle of wine in one hand and two glasses in the other. "Charcuterie board is on the coffee table—extra olives—and the brie is warm."

Reaching for a glass, I toss my earbuds on my bed and ask, "Is he gone?"

He is.

She wouldn't have told me it was safe if he was still here, but I have to ask.

"Sent him on his merry way with a swift kick in the ass." Sasha gives me a proper pour of wine, not the Boone's Farm college-fill that I really want. "There's more, you know—three full bottles plus what we have tucked away for emergencies," she assures me as she walks down the hallway. "Are you going to be okay, Lyla Dupree?"

"I will be, Sasha Keller. I will be." I take a sip of wine and follow her to the couch, settling in front of the ridiculously artistic cheeseboard she crafted. "It was shorter than I thought it'd be, sweeter than I expected, and now it's over. It's time to get back to reality." I shrug my shoulder. Just one, because that's all I can muster right now.

She watches me over the top of her glass as I dig into the warm brie.

"There was nothing about your relationship that wasn't firmly planted in reality," she observes.

"Sash, it was a fling, an unintended one and nothing more. Certainly not a relationship." I laugh, sadly.

I stare out the window at the skyline of New York and try to push my thoughts toward the things I need to do. My shop. The next location.

Anything but Raleigh Jacobs.

Raleigh

I was wrong.

I lashed out.

I didn't think about... Well, I just didn't fucking think.

The panic of losing Matty—of anything happening to him—sent me to a bad place, and I said shit that I shouldn't have. And then I left.

That seems to be becoming way more of a habit than I'd like to admit.

Shit turned ugly with Laney, and I took the farthest assignment my company had available.

If I'm completely honest with myself, things were actually getting too good, too right with Lyla.

Don't get me wrong, I was completely fucking freaked out at the thought of my kid lost, taken, or in any way alone in that big fucking city, but seeing the way Lyla interacted with Matty scared the shit out of me too.

I saw possibilities in that.

I saw a future.

I saw all the things I wanted, but never dreamed I was ready for.

And I fucking walked away out of fear.

I'm nothing but a big fucking pussy still mulling this shit over.

Mentally shaking myself, I tune back into Career Day in Matty's class.

"...and my dad is the smartest. He knows everything, and that's why he lived in New York City and built the subway. And we went to the Central Park Zoo, but it wasn't like the movie at all. And then we went hiking in another zoo and saw the bears. And we had the best pizza and the best hot chocolate, and he knows the lady who makes the best cookies in the whole entire world."

Every single talking point of Matty's intro solidifies Lyla's place, front and center in my mind, not to mention in my heart.

Except for the part about building the subway and

me being smart and me knowing everything. Obviously, I know nothing.

How the hell did this happen? How did I catch these fucking feelings when I was only there for a couple months?

Somehow, I fake my way through my portion of the presentation and get back to work just in time for a fucking subway explosion.

Not a literal one, but project-wise, schedule-wise, the shit hits the fan.

Email after email.

My phone rings the minute it hits the receiver and my cell phone never stops dancing across my desk.

There's not a damn thing I can do but hop a flight to New York and put out this fucking dumpster fire.

The job should have been completed by now. Had I stayed and seen it through to the end, it would be done and over with—but, again—I had to be a pussy and leave.

It's stupid, but the first place I stop on the way to the job site is *Bonne Chatte et Patisserie*.

"Americano, extra shot, and two chocolate croissants,

please. And throw in one of your big brownies too," I say.

I expected Sam to be running the coffee and the register, but it's not her.

Instead, it's an older lady, close to my mother's age but obviously trained by Sam, at least for the most part.

This woman smiles. Something Sam rarely did.

"I haven't seen you in here before. Are you visiting?" she asks, shocking me.

Sam absolutely did not train her on customer interactions.

Clearing my throat, I answer, "Yeah, for work, though I spent a couple months here over the winter. Is Sam here or did Lyla finally kick her and her bad attitude out the door?"

I shove a five in the tip jar because the coffee is amazing, the croissants smell like heaven, and I'm just so damn happy that Lyla made a positive change hiring this woman.

Sam was efficient, but her personality was shit.

"Oh, uh…"

She doesn't get the chance to finish what she was going to say, or maybe she chooses not to when the door from the kitchen swings open in a rush.

Anticipating a sweet smile and a lock of blonde hair that never quite manages to stay in place, I slap what Lyla called my grumpy grin on my face and turn.

Instead of sweet Lyla, Sam and every bit of that shit attitude is glaring at me, and my grin goes straight to grimace.

"I thought you were gone," Sam says, arms crossed, an apron—Lyla's apron—tied around her waist.

"Sam," I say with a nod of my head. "Where's Lyla? I want to—"

Ignoring the line of people stacking up behind me, Sam plants her hands on the counter and proceeds to dress me down like a drill sergeant.

"What you want doesn't count for shit. You don't get to come in here after months of… and then nothing. And just… just… ask for her. No."

"I get it, Sam. I'm sorry. Please just pop back there and let her know I'm here, so I can talk to her. Apologize, and—"

"She gone," Sam says with a lift of her chin. "Left me to run this place, and that being the case, I have the right to refuse service, so get out. Take what you've got and go. Don't come back."

She straightens up off the counter and pushes through to the kitchen, the door swinging in her wake.

"What does she mean, Lyla's gone?" I ask the new barista.

The response is shouted from the kitchen, "She. Doesn't. Work. Here. Gone, asshole. Departed, left. Past whatever-the-fuck of *Go*. And a whole lot of none-of-your-fucking-business."

This exchange has taken far too long, and the people waiting in line for their morning caffeine and sugar fix are getting restless. So I thank the new addition for my coffee, resist the urge to flip off the kitchen door, and I leave.

After a full day of muddling through shitstorm after dumpster fire at the job site, I take a taxi straight to 48th and Lexington.

It looks different. Almost pretty with the evening sun glinting off the chrome.

Technically, I'm still within the terms of my sublet, so I greet Thomas and hit the elevator call button, thankful when it opens right away.

When the doors part on the seventeenth floor, it's as if nothing has changed, and yet everything has changed.

I pause in front of Lyla's door, running my hand down my close-cropped beard before knocking. And while I wait, it doesn't escape my notice that the air is still and bland. Filled with absolutely nothing.

This hallway that always held scents of the most amazing pastries is not just silent, it smells only of air freshener and a hint of wet dog.

Finally, the door opens, and a look of surprise flashes across Sasha's face before it quickly morphs into that of the pissed off best friend.

"What's up… neighbor?" Sasha fills the doorway. Arms crossed over her chest, she's full of righteous indignation.

"Hey. Is, uh… I need to talk to Lyla," I say.

Getting through the best friend is never a guarantee, and I get the distinct feeling that this is going to be the fucking challenge of the century.

"Can I come in?"

She takes her time, thinking hard about how best to answer—whether to kick my ass to the curb or to lay me low.

After already getting shut down by Sam, my chances of making it past Lyla's gatekeepers are not looking good, so with a stiff nod, I take a step back and turn toward the elevator.

"She's not here." Sasha steps aside, making way for me to enter their apartment.

I step through and note that the chair I always used to turn off the smoke alarm is gone. "When will she be back?" I shift my weight from one foot to the other looking through to the living room.

I can't put my finger on anything specific, but it feels different. Looks different.

Sasha rolls her lips into her mouth and blows out a hard breath. "She won't, Raleigh. She's gone. She left New York and went… Well, she went. I can't tell you specifics because that's not my place, but she's moved on to bigger things." She hits me with a serious side-eye. "To better things."

Registering an inexplicable ache, I put my fist to my chest, pushing hard against the pain that's lodged there.

"Where is she, Sasha? Where did she go?" I plead. "Tell me. I need to talk to her. I…"

I honestly don't even know how to express just how badly I want—no, need—to find Lyla. This drive makes no sense, none whatsoever, but I *need* to find her. Can't fucking conceive of not finding her. I have to fucking find her and…

"Again, not for me to say. She's…"

This whole discussion is obviously really uncomfortable for her. I can't quite figure out if it's because she wants to spill all her secrets or because she doesn't.

Either way, there is no mistaking the fact that she's pissed as fuck at me. But Sasha is squirming in her proverbial seat.

With an almost imperceptible nod, Sasha makes up her mind. "Lyla's been fucked over pretty solidly in relationships. Her mother's been up her ass about moving back home after... And she's been resisting it hard, but…"

What does that mean? What does any of this mean?

"Where can I find her, Sasha? Where is she?"

Sasha just shakes her head. "Go home, Raleigh. Just go home. Let her move on and find her happiness in…

Let her just try to find her happiness again." She catches herself before spilling where Lyla is.

With a sad smile, Sasha opens the door for me to leave. And, though it's killing me, I do.

Head down, tail between my legs, I walk out the door.

In the lobby, I'm stopped by the woman who brought Matty back to me the day I lost him. I never did learn her first name, but I think her last name was Hendrix? Henderson?

"Hey, how's your little guy? Is he coming back to visit anytime soon?" she asks kindly.

"No. He's home for good, and I'm done here. Just had to pop back into town and take care of some details." I don't know why I feel the need to explain, but I do. And now, there's nothing left for me but to go home.

I leave my key with Thomas and slip into the back of a cab where I'm hit with a southern twang like I haven't heard since I got to New York the first time.

"Where we headin'?" Sure enough, when he turns to scan for an opening in traffic, it's Roy, the driver who welcomed me to the city.

"La Guardia."

"Starting a vacation or finishing up an adventure?" he asks, a smile still stretched across his face, genuine interest still evident in his voice.

"I'm not sure. Going home, but—"

The car lurches forward into traffic, and we're off.

"But?" he prods, finally glancing at me in the mirror.

I wonder if there's any way he could possibly remember me, but it's been months, and he must have had literally thousands of people in and out of his cab in that time.

"I think I missed my adventure, let it slip through my fingers."

That—right there—is some bullshit, and I know it. I shit all over that adventure and the girl who was sweet enough to play my tour guide.

The cab is absolutely silent, not a word spoken, nothing other than road noise bleeding through the vacuum separating me from the city I never wanted any ties to. The city where I found what I didn't know I was looking for.

As we pull up to the departure gates, eyes that seem to hold the wisdom of the world draw mine to the mirror in the center of the windshield.

"Your adventure is still out there, son, and, if memory serves me, you're no fool. Give it a minute. My guess is she'll find it in her heart to work her way back to you and see this thing through."

I can't help but shake my head at the absolute absurdity of that actually happening.

"But when she does, Denver-boy, you're going to

have to be ready. You only get one second chance." He turns his gaze away from me, staring straight out the windshield.

I pull myself from the back of the taxi, and before I can say thank you, Roy is gone in a blur of yellow taxis.

I chew on his words, let them roll around in my head as I check into my flight and wait through the interminable security line.

It's not until I'm seated at my gate and the airline attendant makes the announcement that the flight to Denver will begin boarding in five minutes that …

Denver.

Denver.

Out of all the faces and fares Roy's seen since the beginning of the year, he remembered me. Remembered not just my face, but that I'm from Denver.

I feel like fucking Cinderella, and my fairy godmother is none other than a slow-talking, New York City cab driver from Alabama.

Eighteen

Lyla

"Thanks, Mom. Yep. Uh-huh, uh-huh."

With a flour-dusted hand, I wedge my phone deeper into the shrug of my shoulder. I should just break down and buy new earbuds, but as soon as I do, I'll find the box that mine are hiding in.

There's no use trying to get a word in edgewise when my mom calls each morning. Our rocky relationship is mending. Slowly—because there were a lot of years that things were rough and we didn't really talk—but it's getting better.

Every day.

Every phone call.

Every conversation that inevitably ends with her telling me she loves me, and she's just so glad that I'm finally home.

"I love you, Lyla. Thank you for coming home, Short-cake," she says, using my childhood nickname.

"Love you too. I'm going to stay at work a little later today, and then I've got some apartments lined up to look at."

"No need to rush things, Lyla. Take your time. We love having you here."

I'm thankful for my parents letting me stay in my old bedroom while getting things off the ground with *Bonne Chatte, Deux*, but it's time.

Going from a luxury high-rise in the heart of Manhattan, where I had my own en suite, to sharing a bathroom with my younger brothers for the past couple of weeks has been more than enough. I'm ready for a change.

"I'll see you later, Mom," I say.

The phone slips from its perch and clatters noisily to the floor.

"You okay in here?" my new Sam asks, swinging the kitchen door open—because yes, I moved a couple thousand miles west, opened a new patisserie and still have a front-of-house employee named Sam.

This one's not near as crass as the New York version, but she's at least as good, if not better than New York Sam as a barista.

"Yep, just dropped my phone, nothing important."

I scoop it up off the floor, ignoring the lock screen picture of me dancing with Matty at the Central Park Zoo.

Raleigh sent it to me that night, and I immediately made it the first thing I'd see every time I pick up my phone.

For the gazillionth time this week alone, I think that I should change it, that I'm going to change it. But I won't, not yet.

Dusting the flour from my phone case, I set it on the shelf by the sink and wash my hands. I give the faucet an extra twist because of the drip that—no matter how many times I call the plumber—never seems to stop. Then, I freeze in my tracks.

A voice filters through from the front of the shop. One that lights my insides on fire and stops my heart from beating all at the same time.

"…got my morning coffee at a place like this when I was living in Manhattan. Do you have any chocolate croissants?"

Of course I knew that our paths could cross, eventually. I just didn't really prepare myself for it. I mean, Denver is a big city.

My storefront is nowhere near the office building that houses Raleigh's engineering firm and nowhere near his house.

I know this because I checked. I chose this specific location, that was out of the way, for the very purpose of *not* running into him.

"Sorry, we don't make them," Sam answers kindly. "Though it is kind of weird not to have those, specifically in a French bakery. I'd be happy to make the suggestion for you."

She has. On more than one occasion, Sam has told me we need chocolate croissants, that people ask for them all the time.

"Sweet. Thanks." Raleigh grunts slightly and adds, "Never thought I'd say it, but I miss the taste of them. It reminds me of home. I mean, New York. See you tomorrow."

Seconds later, the bell above the door jingles, announcing his departure. I count to twenty before peeking out to make sure the coast is clear.

New Sam glances over her shoulder as she wipes down the already clean countertop and smiles broadly at me. "Another request for—"

"I heard." My voice is shaky, even with just those two little words. Her face screws up, and I wave her concern away. "What… what did that guy look like?" I ask even though I know in my heart that it was him.

Sam sighs with little cartoon hearts in her eyes. "He was yummy, Lyla. Tall, dark hair and the perfect beard, not scraggly and out of control like some of the mountain men around here, but just enough to tickle a girl's"—her cheeks go bright pink—"Oh God, sorry. That was totally inappropriate. I shouldn't have said that out loud, certainly not about a customer."

Such a difference from New York Sam.

I chuckle and pour myself a coffee. "No worries," I tell her, looking out the front window.

"He said he'd be back tomorrow though. Want me to drop an empty tray, so you have a reason to run out and feast your eyes on him yourself?" she offers.

History is being a pushy bitch.

"No, I'm good. Thanks for looking out for me though."

With a last look out to the sunny sidewalk, I go back to the kitchen and try to focus on prepping for lunch. The day passes in an easy rhythm, and when two o'clock rolls around, I let Sam go for the afternoon.

"You sure you don't want me to stay? What if you get slammed?" She worries at a nonexistent spot on the glass display case.

"It's fine. I'll manage," I assure her. We do a steady business, but nothing like the chaos of the New York shop.

Honestly, if I hustled, I could handle this location entirely on my own. I just like having the security of another set of hands, and I've found that I kind of like the slower pace.

"Okay," she draws the word out, adding the non-verbal *if you're sure*.

I nod and send her on her way, locking the door and flipping the sign to *Closed* as soon as she's out of sight.

I need a minute.

I need therapy.

I need to bake.

Back in the kitchen, I pour myself a glass of wine and connect my playlist to the little speaker I have for when I'm alone. *Home* by Edward Sharpe & The Magnetic Zeros will take the lead in the soundtrack of my afternoon.

A couple of hours later, I sit in my car on a street I've avoided like the plague, in front of a house that I swore I wouldn't stalk. But here I am.

I should start my car and go look at apartments.

I should go back to my parents' house and see what my mom made for dinner.

I should text him and see if…

If what? The whole reason I'm here is to ask the question that has been swirling around my brain since he walked away.

And if I chicken out?

I won't. *I won't.*

I push myself from my car and walk around the front to take the things I need from the passenger seat.

The late afternoon sun warms my back, and I set

everything on the hood of my SUV, twisting my hair back into a messy bun on the top of my head. It's not like it looked good down after being pulled back all day anyway. My hair being up or down isn't going to impact how this goes.

Bracing myself, I grab my stuff and approach the dark blue bungalow. It's cuter than I expected. White trim, a bright yellow front door, neatly trimmed shrubs, a boy's bike leaning against the side of the garage.

My knock spurs high pitched barking—not the yap of a small dog, but that of a puppy that promises to be a big manly dog in a house of bachelors. A dog for a father and son, one that simply says *home*.

"Marty, knock it off," drifts through the closed door, and when it opens, revealing a fat, brindled pit-bull puppy clutched tightly to Raleigh's chest, I melt a little bit on the inside.

Subtle stripes and big white paws, a pink nose, and the biggest sloppiest smile are enough to distract me for a heartbeat. Just one, though, because when my name spills from Raleigh's lips, all my focus goes straight to him.

"Lyla." The way his tongue rolls over the *Ls*, caressing each tiny syllable, sends shivers down my spine. "Come in, please. Let me just put Marty in her kennel." He opens the door and hurries into the house with the squirming pup.

A sound like nothing I've ever heard follows him back into the comfortable looking living room.

"Sorry, she's got a lot of personality and likes to share it. I swear, the only thing aggressive about pitties are the way they snuggle and their need to do it constantly. And on their terms."

The mournful baying continues, getting more and more pitiful with every squawk.

"She'll stop eventually," Raleigh says, glancing over his shoulder at an even more insistent yowl.

"Are you sure?" I follow his gaze.

He turns back toward me, running a hand through his thick brown hair, messing it up adorably. "No. Not at all. I think she'll keep going until I let her out. Do you mind?"

He looks as pained as poor little Marty sounds.

"Nope. Go set her free."

In no time, the scrape of toenails on hardwood fills the air as little Marty barrels around the corner. She slides into me, pushing me off balance.

"Sorry. She's small, but packs a lot of punch," Raleigh says, steadying me.

Electricity sparks along my skin where his hands grip my shoulders.

He lets go far too soon, and I feel the loss deeply.

An awkward moment hangs between us, neither of us taking the lead in this dance.

Marty sits on my left foot and leans into me hard, threatening to knock me off balance again.

"Maybe we should sit." Raleigh puts his hand out toward the leather couch, and Marty makes a run for it, executing a perfect flying leap that lands her right in the middle of the deep cushion, tail wagging, cheeks stretched in a broad smile.

I follow, sitting at one end of the couch where she promptly flops down half on top of me.

Miles of vacant leather and she's *right there.*

"I think she likes me," I say, resting the bakery box on my knees and scratching her neck rolls. In no time at all, her eyes are closed and snores that outsize her body rumble through the room.

"She has good taste."

I still my hand and look up at where Raleigh stands in front of me.

There are so many things running through my mind. So many things I want to say. To ask.

I smash my lips together and force my hurt to back down.

Being a snarky bitch has never gotten me where I wanted to be. That's what the bubbly personality is for. But right now, I want honest answers to honest questions. I just don't know where to start.

"I went back to New York," he says softly, settling awkwardly into the chair to my right.

"I thought you said there would never be anything that could get you to go back there," I say. It's not a question, and it's certainly not bubbly.

"Turns out, I was wrong." He shifts, turning to face me just a little bit more. "There were things I found in Manhattan that grew on me, things that, when I came back home, I missed. A lot."

A muscle in his jaw jumps as he works his jaw from side to side. "You know, I haven't had a decent cup of coffee since I left… until today."

"Really?" We're dancing again, neither of us quite ready to jump into what needs to be addressed.

Raleigh nods and smiles softly as his gaze darts around the room, finally resting on where his dog is snuggled tight against me.

"Yep. It's a great little place on my way to work from Matty's school. Kind of glad I found it today. It's almost perfect."

I arch a brow at him.

"Not quite, but almost," he clarifies, looking up through his thick lashes and into my eyes.

"And what would make it perfect?"

He drops his gaze to the square box tied up with red and white string resting on my knees.

I place the box in his hands and watch as he carefully picks at the string. "I went to the *Bonne Chatte* when I was in New York. I went back to your apartment, too.

Neither Sam nor Sasha would tell me anything, just that you'd left."

"I did. It was time to make my move on expanding." We had touched on the possibility of me opening a second location.

Raleigh nods, absently sliding the string through his fingers. "I thought you were leaning toward Minneapolis."

Uncertainty weaves through his words and pulls at his brows.

"I was. But I decided it was time for me to come home." As the words leave my mouth, Marty grunts and pushes herself up and fully onto my lap.

"Marty," he scolds. "Sorry, she's going to get fur on that." He places the box on the coffee table and tries to remove his dog from where she's sprawled across the second item I brought for Raleigh. "Damn, she's practically glued to you. Let me just—"

"It's okay. Actually, it's your t-shirt," I tell him, pulling the soft gray shirt out from under Marty.

I hold it between my hands, thinking of all the nights I've fallen asleep with it clutched to my chest or tucked under my pillow. The nights I slept wrapped up in it just to feel closer to him.

"I accidentally stole it when I was helping you pack your bags."

Raleigh cringes at the mention of him fleeing New

York. His cheeks go pink, and he rubs his hand over his beard, the scrape of his whiskers against his palm rasping through the room.

"I thought today might be a good day to return it to you." I nod, pushing the shirt toward him.

It hangs in the space between us, but Raleigh makes no move to reach for it.

"I don't—"

"It's one that you wore a lot, so I figure you've probably missed it. I'm sorry I kept it for so long. That wasn't cool of me." I thrust it closer to him, but he doesn't take it.

Instead, Raleigh wraps his hands around mine—holding them reverently between his warm palms—as he slides down to kneel on the floor in front of me.

"I don't give a fuck about that t-shirt. I missed you, Lyla. You were the bright spot in that dingy city, and when I left, those clouds seemed to follow me home. The sun only started shining again when I walked into a new coffee shop today."

Nineteen

Raleigh

My heart feels like it could explode.

Lyla's in Denver.

She's in my house.

She's here, and I'm more than likely going to screw this up.

It's what I do.

"I missed you too," she whispers. "But I need to know what this is—what it was. If there actually was something between us."

I take the t-shirt from her and place it on the couch, where Marty the wonder-pit paws at it until she's flopped over and has it snuggled up under her chin.

I shake my head at the goofy dog that Matty named after the zebra that he absolutely did not see at the Central Park Zoo.

He claimed that her striping made her look like the obnoxious character, and since it was his favorite day ever—even though he didn't get to see any of the animals from the movie—her name *had* to be Marty. Because I wouldn't allow him to give her the name he really wanted.

Lyla. It's just not right to name a snoring, farting dog after such a beautiful woman.

When Marty's settled, I take one of Lyla's hands in each of mine, holding them firmly between us. "There was absolutely something," I tell her. "There still is. I don't know exactly how to label it after all this time, but it's something I want to investigate. Explore more deeply. I want a second chance at this, at us. To see where things go and what else there is that's yet to be discovered. I can't promise you sunshine and fairytales every day, but I want a chance. I don't want to walk away from this. And I will forever regret that I did. I'm so sorry."

"Raleigh," she says my name on a whisper.

"Please, Lyla. Forgive me—I fucked up in New York. I panicked over losing Matty, and I was an ass. I'll do things right this time. Woo you, date you. Show you all the best parts of *my* city. We can go hiking in the mountains, walk hand in hand down the city's streets. I'll take you to the Denver Zoo, and the one in Colorado Springs. I'll cook for you and surprise you with home ice hockey tickets," I plead.

"Raleigh," she says it a little bit stronger, but I'm not done.

I don't think I've said enough to convince her. How can I make up for all the shitty things I said to her in New York? For losing my mind and just walking away.

"I want to show you all my favorite places, remind you what snow is supposed to look like, how the air is supposed to smell. Take you camping. Sit and listen to the sounds of nature, to the beauty of silence all around you, and—"

"Raleigh, stop." Lyla's demand cuts me short, but the minute I look into her eyes, I forget whatever I was about to say. And when her lips crash against mine, I don't give a flying fuck about those forgotten words.

I slide my hand to her neck, my thumb under her chin, tilting her head, so I can return the kiss. I pull at the band in her hair until the mass of blonde waves tumble down around her shoulders.

She tastes as sweet as I remember, as perfect as ever. I could die a happy man from the taste of her lips alone.

Lyla scoots to the edge of the couch and pulls me close until I'm nestled between her thighs.

There's no place I'd rather be.

She grips my back in one hand, the other twisting

and twining through my hair. Nipping and biting at my lips.

"Lyla," I groan as she slides off the couch, so we're both kneeling in front of it. Chest to chest, wrapped up in each other's arms.

I shuffle back, giving her space, not because I want it, but because I want to do this thing between us the right way this time. I rushed into things in New York, and then fucked them up at every turn. I want this time to be different, less primal and right now, and a whole lot more of just plain *right*.

She pushes against my chest until I fall—ass on the floor, my back against the chair. And then Lyla, sweet Lyla, swings a leg across my hips, straddling me.

Her hair hangs around us like a curtain. She rolls her hips, sliding her core over my dick—and I swear to God—I have to recite building code and engineering principals to keep from jizzing in my pants like a fucking teenager.

I want her.

I want her fiercely.

But I want her to know that I truly want more.

With my hands on either side of her neck, I slow the kiss and calm the frenzy buzzing through me.

"Lyla, wait, sweet girl. Slow down. We don't have to—"

She leans back, brow cocked, smirk in place.

"Raleigh," she says, her voice low, hips shimmying and rubbing me in all the right places. Driving me out of my fucking mind. "Are you telling me you want me to stop?"

In fact, I do not want her to stop. I don't want her to stop at all. I want her to stay here, pressed against me and in my arms. Forever.

"Hell, no, but… Did you hear what I just said? I want more with you. I want—"

"I want that too, Raleigh, I do. But this"—she rotates her hips and every muscle in my body clenches —"I missed you." She leans in and kisses me. "I want *you*."

She crosses her arms and grabs the hem of her bold pink t-shirt. Pulling it over her head, she tosses it over her shoulder to the couch.

Suddenly, Marty snorts and sneezes, rolling around on the cushion like the little drama queen she is until she's wrapped up in Lyla's shirt, head resting on my gray one with just her little pink nose showing between the folded cotton. And then the snoring amps up to a whole new level.

Lyla's entire body vibrates with laughter as she drops her head to my chest. The feeling is decidedly not unpleasant because her shaky giggles are jiggling my junk, and there's not a damn thing wrong with that.

"Oh my God, either your dog is stealing the show, or

my seduction skills are terrible," she manages to say between those snickers.

With my hands to her hips, I try to hold her still because blowing my load like this is just fucking wrong.

"Legendarily terrible. Alarmingly so," I mumble against the crown of her head.

"Alarming? You should have absolutely nothing against my alarm. It's what got us here."

Lyla lifts her head, raising her gaze to meet mine. Her radiant smile lights up the room.

How did a grumpy bastard like me get so damn lucky?

How is it that—after the shit I pulled—she's here?

In my house.

On my lap.

"I'm pretty sure it was actually my alarm that got us *here*." I rock my hips, thrusting my hips up, grinding my dick against her core. "You didn't happen to bring any of that gooey chocolate in the bag, did you?" I reach for the pastry box on the coffee table.

"I didn't, but I did bring you a treat." She pulls the string from the box, and when the lid opens, one more positive thing from my time in Manhattan clicks into place.

"Do you still have to bake constantly to keep your neighbors from being pissed off?" I ask. "How is it that no one complained about your alarm there? Complained and got you booted from the building?"

Lyla rips off a piece of flakey pastry and holds it up to my mouth. I lean in and take the chocolatey croissant from her fingers, grazing my teeth along her skin as I do.

It's meant to be sexy.

It's meant to turn her on.

My singular goal is to drive her fucking insane.

Instead, Marty picks that moment to perk up, deciding she needs to be involved. And she woofs and bays and makes the most god-awful noise that only her breed is capable of, killing all the sexy vibes.

Murdering them, really.

"Oh my God, your dog is a mess." Lyla laughs, climbing off my lap and sauntering down the hall toward the bedrooms. The sway of her hips is sweet and seductive.

"Stay." I point to Marty, praying that she's content enough in her t-shirt fort, and then happily follow Lyla to show her just how happy I am to have her home.

Twenty

T he whistle blows, and the referee throws his hand toward the net, arm straight, knife-hand in full effect.

Matty wobbles on his skates as he tries his very hardest to pull off the victory move he's been practicing since we signed him up for ice hockey. He gets his balance back, but just barely.

Finally, he gives up on the theatrics and skates down the line getting high fives from his teammates and coaches for his very first goal.

He's come close to scoring, but nerves, anticipation

and genuine excitement were piling up on him, and the poor kid thought he'd be the only one not to score this season.

Now that it's happened, he's so damn pumped, he skates down the opposing team's bench and gets high-fives from all of them as well.

Hockey at this age is a different beast. Slow and boring as hell unless it's your kid's team giving it everything they've got and playing for the love of the game.

And the snacks. These kids are all about the after-game snacks.

Too soon, parents and pressure and bullying and aggression will change the dynamics, but for now, every single person here is excited for the kid who just put the puck in the net.

When the buzzer sounds, and the exhibition game is done, I head to the locker room to help Matty with his skates.

He still likes to keep his pads on for as long as possi-ble, stinking up the car on the way home. But today, he's got most of his gear off and is tugging on his little Avalanche jersey, his head already popping through as I round the corner.

Raleigh was torn between filming Matty's game from the stands or hanging out in the crowded tunnel with a crappy view of the ice.

"Did you see my goal? Did you?" Matty's voice rises

above the noise of the make-shift locker room. "I did it just like we practiced. Just like you taught me."

"You're right, buddy. I knew you had it in you." I bump knuckles with him because the last thing I want to do is embarrass him in front of his friends.

My concerns are short-lived because as soon as I get close enough, he stands up and throws his arms around me, hugging me tight.

"Thanks, Lyla. You're the best," he says, releasing me and shoving his gear into his bag. It's almost the same size as him, and I laugh as he leans so far forward to get the weight off the ground, his chest is almost parallel to the ground. "Did Dad see my goal? Did he get a video? I totally wanna see it. I did the thing, and then it flew— did you see how it flew through everybody? It was so fast. I can't *wait* 'til I can do slap shots. Slap shots are so cool, right Lyla?" Matty rambles away as he makes his way to the door.

His huge bag sways back and forth, nearly toppling him over with each step.

"Matty, leave your stuff here. We'll get it after the game's done." I help him set the oversized backpack against the wall and tuck his stick—his goal maker—in behind it.

Matty watches me, silently chewing on his cheek. "What if someone *steals* it?" he whispers, reaching for his stick. "It's got goals in it now."

It takes everything I have not to bust out laughing, and I absolutely can't.

Matty is so damn serious right now, and I have to respect that.

"It'll be fine. I promise. See?" I point to the security guard at the end of the tunnel opposite where the Zamboni is clearing the ice.

The hard-carving edges of the U-6 hockey teams' skates are being erased, the ice returning to a perfectly mirrored surface.

And the only evidence of Matty's first goal scored—let alone in a professional arena filled with die-hard Colorado fans—is hopefully on Raleigh's phone.

"Let's go find your dad and see that video."

We wind our way through the arena and back to the unbelievable ice-level seats Raleigh paid a mint for as soon as he found out there was a possibility of his son playing in the exhibition game. He didn't give me a dollar amount when I asked how much they were. He just replied that it's not every day that your kid plays between periods on professional ice.

I love how he loves his son.

I love how he loves me.

"Dad, lemme see it. Was it the best? It was the best, right?"

Matty jumps into the seat next to Raleigh and reaches for his phone.

Knowing full well that there's no getting past this, Raleigh queues up the video and hands his phone to Matty.

"That's the awesomest. Did you send it to Mom already?" Without taking his eyes from the screen, he replays the video clip as he crouches down, mimicking his victory move in the narrow space between his dad and me.

"I did. Sent it as soon as you were off the ice." Raleigh looks at me over Matty's head and rolls his eyes.

"I wish she could've been here for it," Matty mumbles. Never taking his eyes from Raleigh's phone, he starts the clip back up from the beginning.

Laney could have been here to see Matty play. She was supposed to be, promised her son that she would be here. But just as she did when I first ran into her in New York as she left Matty in the high-rise's lobby with a complete stranger, Laney proved herself an unreliable flake again.

Instead, she signed her custodial right over to Raleigh, packed up her stuff and moved out of state last month.

As much as Raleigh hated the Big Apple, his ex-wife decided she loved everything about it. So, while she's off living her best life and chasing her man of the month, I get to be here, back in my hometown, reconnecting with my parents and siblings.

Even better, I get to make memories and live the adventure called life with a rambunctious pit bull and my two amazing guys.

Thank you so much for reading Sweet on You! I love Raleigh,
but also realize that this is a bit of a departure from my norm.
To stay up on all of my book news, make sure to sign up for my newsletter to get the inside scoop!

Playlist

Home-Edward Sharpe & The Magnetic Zeros
Sick of Losing Soulmates-dodie
Hard Feelings/Loveless-Lorde
Nice to Meet Ya-Niall Horan
I Will Be Okay-Mimi Bay
My Thoughts on You-The Band CAMINO
I Fall Apart-Wild Fire
Stay-5 Seconds of Summer
Honey I'm Sorry-Joel Leggett

Acknowledgments

This book was hard. Really hard, and there is no way I could have finished it if not for some truly amazing people in my life.

My husband. We spent the last two years geographically separated and then, in the midst of writing this, made a major move. Uprooted our lives, one kid and our dogs, leaving another kid behind. It hasn't been easy, but we're home again.

Deedy Hays. We talked plot. She kept me sane and did a whole lot of figuratively patting my hair and telling me it was going to be okay. I have plot notes on the backs of receipts from Book Bonanza, countless messages and phone calls. Raleigh and Lyla wouldn't be here without her.

Stacy Garcia. Thank you for reading SoY and pulling teasers. Then, as only Stacy can do, she took those teaser lines and made the most amazing graphics to go with them.

Marie Saunders. Read the unpolished story of Raleigh and Lyla and gave me great insight and suggestions.

Many thanks to all the bloggers and readers, to everyone who has read and reviewed.

And to all my friends in my reader group, McBride's on Main, you are amazing! Thank you for your dedication and patience over the past year or so. Man, it's been rough, but with your laughs, your live videos and continued support, we are back on track. There are great things coming, so grab yourselves a drink and settle in.